"Here—let me help you." Ty lifted the helmet off her head and reached around to release her hair. He could feel her breath on his neck.

Michelle bent her torso away from him. "What're you doing?"

"Trying to get your head in this helmet. Your hair is stopping it from going on."

"Oh."

"What did you think I was doing? Making a play for you?"

"No."

"Yes, you did." He looked her straight in the eyes, wishing the streetlights were brighter. "If and when I make a play for you, you won't need to question what I'm doing. It will be perfectly clear."

Dear Reader

I've always been fascinated by the attraction between two people. So many times men and woman are complete opposites and still find that special spark. A good-looking man and an unattractive woman, or the reverse. The introvert and the extrovert. The super-popular person and the one in the corner. The person who loves adventure and the one who prefers to watch TV. It amazes me how humans manage to pair off.

These extreme differences are what I explore in Michelle and Ty's story. They couldn't be more dissimilar and yet they fit—complement each other as if they are puzzle pieces finding their spot. What made writing this book especially fun was watching the two characters squirm as they find that they truly do belong together.

I would be remiss if I didn't mention and thank Dr Bruce Miller, who is an anaesthesiologist extraordinaire. Much of Ty's doctoring skills and sensitive interactions with patients were influenced through knowing Dr Miller and witnessing him in action. I also have to say a big thanks to Dr Kirk Kanter, a heart surgeon with a big heart. There is none better in the world. Through him I received amazing technical assistance that helped Michelle's world become real. All doctors should be as good and as dedicated as these two men are to their patients.

I hope you enjoyed reading Michelle and Ty's story as much as I enjoyed writing it. I love to hear from my readers. You can contact me at www.SusanCarlisle.com.

Susan

THE REBEL DOC WHO STOLE HER HEART

BY
SUSAN CARLISLE

Published in Great Britain 2014
by Mills & Boon, an imprint of Harlequin (UK) Limited,
Eton House, 18-24 Paradise Road, Richmond, Surrey, TW9 1SR

© 2014 Susan Carlisle

ISBN: 978 0 263 24358 1

Susan Carlisle's love affair with books began when she made a bad grade in math in the sixth grade. Not allowed to watch TV until she'd brought the grade up, she filled her time with books and became a voracious romance reader. She has 'keepers' on the shelf to prove it. Because she loved the genre so much she decided to try her hand at creating her own romantic worlds. She still loves a good happily-ever-after story.

When not writing Susan doubles as a high school substitute teacher, which she has been doing for sixteen years. Susan lives in Georgia with her husband of twenty-eight years and has four grown children. She loves castles, travelling, cross-stitching, hats, James Bond and hearing from her readers.

Recent titles by the same author:

SNOWBOUND WITH DR DELECTABLE
NYC ANGELS: THE WALLFLOWER'S SECRET*
HOT-SHOT DOC COMES TO DOWN
THE NURSE HE SHOULDN'T NOTICE
HEART SURGEON, HERO...HUSBAND?

NYC Angels

**These books are also available in eBook format
from www.millsandboon.co.uk**

To Andy, the Mr Romance in my life.
I love you.

**Praise for
Susan Carlisle:**

'Susan Carlisle pens her romances beautifully…
HOT-SHOT DOC COMES TO TOWN is a book
that I would recommend not only to Medical Romance
fans but to anyone looking to curl up with an
angst-free romance about taking a chance
and following your heart.'
—*HarlequinJunkie.com*

CHAPTER ONE

HEART SURGEON MICHELLE ROSS used her hip to nudge open the swinging door to the number four operating room in Raleigh Medical Center in North Carolina.

Her patient, Mr. Martin, waiting on her to begin repairing his artery, was the type of person that affected her most. There were almost always young children waiting at home for their parent to get better. She had to save this father. Make sure he lived to return to his family.

Dressed in sterile gown and with hands covered in latex gloves, she eyed her team and asked in a crisp voice, "Are we ready to begin?"

The quietly speaking group gathered around the middle-aged patient suddenly became mute. If a scalpel had been mishandled and fallen to the floor it would have echoed in the soundless room.

She looked at each of them and watched as every set of eyes refused to meet her gaze. What was going on? Normally her team was ready to proceed without hesitation. She asked the same question before each operation out of habit.

Glitches weren't allowed in her OR. Efficiency was her motto. Her patients deserved the best and she saw that they got it. She'd hand-picked her team and they knew what was expected, she trusted them, so what was the issue?

Her team's unwillingness to answer didn't alleviate her

anxiety over a case that would require her complete attention. She stepped to her place beside the table before her gaze landed on the *anesthesiologist resident* at the head of the patient. "Where's Schwartzie?" she demanded.

The younger doctor's eyes flickered a couple of times above the top edge of his surgical mask and he said, "Dr. Schwartz's replacement isn't here yet."

Annoyance blistered in her. Her patient deserved better. She opened her mouth to respond but someone entering the door stopped her. A man with wide shoulders had his back to her. He made an agile pivot and faced the group. A bright orange zebra-striped surgical cap screamed for attention in her sterile and ordered world. The basic blue surgical uniform of the hospital covered his body but what caught her attention again were the glowing lime-colored clogs that shone through the surgical paper booties on his feet.

Who was this clown? All that was missing was the red nose. As he approached the group her focus centered on his striking jade-colored eyes above his mask. Those orbs met hers expectantly, held her gaze before the twinkle in them put her off guard.

Surely this wasn't her missing anesthesiologist?

"Hey, I'm Ty Smith. I'm filling in for Schwartz." Despite the mask covering his mouth, she could tell he was smiling as he made eye contact with each person.

"We have a patient waiting," she said, halting any further pleasantries.

"You must be Dr. Ross," he stated in a cheerful tone.

"I am. And I'm ready to begin."

He pulled the stool forward with his foot and sat with one easy movement. He didn't seem to give her a further thought or show any concern that they had all been waiting for him.

Looking at the resident, he said, "Nicely done."

The young man who had been so flustered by her question earlier visibly relaxed.

Dr. Smith checked the anesthesia set-up and looked at her. "Ready when you are, Doc."

Once again his eyes caught her off guard. They reminded her of a spring lawn after a rain they were so green. She couldn't let him divert her attention from the patient. She never forgot her duty. "It's Dr. Ross," she corrected.

"Patient is ready, Dr. Ross." He said her name with a subtle twist that implied he might be making fun of her.

Hours later, as she began making the final sutures, Michelle was pleased the procedure had gone without a glitch. Her patient would live a long time and get to see his children grow up. Of that she was particularly proud.

Her father had died of a heart attack when she'd been twelve. They'd been out shopping for new school clothes, something she and her mother hadn't been able to agree on, when he'd clutched his chest and fallen to the floor of the mall. She could still hear the yells to call 911 and the running of feet, but mostly it was the sound of her own crying that she remembered.

At the funeral, as she'd sat beside her mother in the front pew of the church, she'd vowed that she'd help ensure that as many children as possible never experienced what she had. Her answer had been to study and work hard to become a heart surgeon. Her personal experience had taught her there was no room for humor here. This was serious business.

Michelle was in the process of closing when a soft hum, which began at the head of the table, distracted her. During the operation she hadn't looked at the new guy. Instead, she had given Mr. Martin her complete attention, even when her surgical resident had been making the opening incision. She glanced toward the head of the table to find Dr. Smith busily studying a monitor. The others around the table shifted restlessly. As far as she was concerned, the OR was no place for music. She wanted nothing to distract their concentration. She'd always seen to it that any noise remained at a minimum.

Tension as thick as the polar icecap and just as cold filled the space. She didn't miss the covert glances directed her way or towards the humming man.

The new guy looked up, his gaze meeting hers. The lines around his eyes crinkled. "You can join in if you wish."

The man was too disrupting to her OR. He had to go. She'd see that he wasn't assigned to her cases again. "How's the BP?" she asked in a crisp voice.

"Holding steady," he responded.

"Then let's finish this up and get him to CICU. And no more humming."

"Yes, ma'am."

He sounded like a mischievous fourth-grade boy who'd just gotten into trouble for pulling a girl's hair. Not very sincere and determined to do it again.

Ty rubbed the back of his neck to ease his strained muscles as he stepped out of the OR. Having traveled most of the night to arrive on time, he was tired. The car accident he'd assisted with at the city limits hadn't made the situation any better. He didn't like being late but it couldn't be helped. He'd been the first one on the scene and it had been necessary to stay. He took his oath as a doctor seriously.

Moving from one place to another didn't bother him. Heck, he'd done it all his life. That had been one of the problems. His parents had been follow-the-band, sixties wannabe hippies who'd had no business having children but they had. Joey, his younger brother by six years, had needed to stay in one place and have stable medical care but that hadn't been for his parents. They had sought help from this guru here, a herb there or "If we only lived in the desert climate" Joey could breathe better—get better. They had been wrong. Dead wrong.

His parents had said it was just how it was supposed to be. For him, Joey being alive and pestering him about wanting to follow him somewhere was how it should have been. Sitting on the ground in the middle of the moaning and groaning and incense-smoke rising, Ty had decided that he couldn't live like that any more.

He hadn't been able to accept that his parents had refused to take Joey to a traditional doctor. That he'd not done so himself. He'd let Joey die. That had been when he'd made the decision to leave the community and go and live with his grandparents.

He was intelligent enough and with excellent grades he'd decided to attended med school. Maybe by helping others he could make amends for what had happened to his brother. Just out of med school he'd been offered a job by a friend who had been starting up a company supplying fill-in doctors to hospitals. He'd taken it. As a supply doctor he'd gone wherever he'd been needed, normally only staying a few weeks in each place. He was familiar with that type of lifestyle. But right now all he wanted was to find the apartment he'd been promised and fall into bed.

"Dr...."

"Ty Smith." He offered his hand to the woman surgeon he'd shared the OR with.

She was a looker. Shiny brown hair, rosebud lips, and creamy skin. Too bad she had such an abrasive personality. She was a stuffed shirt if he'd ever met one. He'd met a number of them over the years, but this one took the prize.

"We haven't been formally introduced. I go by Ty. What may I call you?"

"Dr. Ross."

Brr...a cold wind. Even the color of her eyes fit her attitude. Normally he was a sucker for a woman with clear blue pools for eyes, but not this time. He'd worked with others who hadn't been completely comfortable with his less than "buttoned-up" ways but she was the iciest to date. No warm welcome here.

"May I speak to you a moment? Privately," she said, in one of the primmest tones he'd ever heard.

"Certainly." He stepped towards a quiet corner and she followed.

Finding his best professional voice, he said, "Well...Dr. Ross, it is a pleasure to meet you. I look forward to working with you."

"That isn't going to happen again. I don't think we're right for each other. I expect my anesthesiologist to be punctual."

What had happened to put such a chip on this woman's shoulder?

"I'm sorry you feel that way. I wasn't intentionally late. And the resident was more than capable of putting the patient under. Our patient was in no danger. So, no harm. No foul. See you around, Dr. Ross." He wanted her to understand that just because he was new to the hospital it didn't mean he couldn't stand his ground.

She sputtered in her effort to respond.

Ty didn't wait to hear what she came up with. He turned and headed towards the locker room to change his clothes.

Two hours later, Ty sat behind the nurses' station in the CICU. He'd not managed to get away as soon as he'd hoped. Busy making notes on the latest patient's chart, he looked up to see Dr. Ross enter, along with a woman and a couple of teenagers. Dr. Ross led the way to Mr. Martin's bed.

The nurse sitting to his left muttered to the clerk on her right, "Well, I see the ice queen has arrived."

So he wasn't special. She was cool to everyone.

"Yeah, but the woman sure can dress," the clerk responded. "Too bad she isn't as nice as her clothes."

These women were jealous.

He couldn't blame them. Dr. Ross was a stately woman with regal bearing. Dressed in a form-fitting pale pink suit jacket and skirt that left no curve untouched, she was eye-catching. He sat up taller in the chair. From his vantage point he could see her from head to toe. He perused her trim calves, following their well-defined length until he stopped at heels that perfectly matched her suit. He'd bet his motorcycle that they were designer, hand-made shoes.

His gaze returned to her dark sable-colored hair. It was pulled back and held by a large silver clasp, which added to the woman-in-control look. She had certainly been hiding some fetching bends and turns under that surgical garb. Too bad that if you touched her with a wet finger it might stick because she was so cold.

She spoke with gracefully arcing hands, pointing and gesturing to pumps and machinery encircling the patient's bed. She must be explaining what they were and how they worked. To his surprise, occasionally she gave the small group a reassuring smile. So there was some warmth under that freezing exterior. She just didn't choose to share it with him.

She glanced toward the desk and for a second her gaze met his. Did he see anxiety in those eyes?

No, that would be the last emotion he'd attribute to Dr. Ross. Self-confidence oozed from her.

Sliding back the chair, Ty continued to watch the family

as they hovered around the patient. Dr. Ross no longer stood in the center of the group. She now blended into the background as she answered an occasional question. Standing, Ty came around the desk, planning to leave the unit. When she looked in his direction again he changed his angle and walked towards the group. Stopping beside her, he asked in hushed tones, "Is there a problem?"

She stiffened. "No. Why would you ask that?" she hissed.

Her eyes were on the family members, as if she was making sure they didn't overhear their conversation.

"Good. From my end he looks good. I don't see any reason the tube can't be pulled out tomorrow morning if he continues on this path."

"I appreciate—"

Her remark was interrupted by the woman he assumed was their patient's wife. She looked at him and then back at Dr. Ross.

The sound of Dr. Ross clearing her throat and the almost imperceptible hesitation didn't get past him but only because he was standing so close to her. She'd had no intention of introducing him but now if she didn't she would appear impolite.

Ty smiled at the woman and extended his hand. "Hi, I'm Ty Smith, I'm the anesthesiologist who worked with Dr. Ross on Mr. Martin's case."

"Thank you for taking such good care of my husband. Our family, my son and daughter…" the woman nodded toward the teens "…are grateful for everything you've done."

"I assure you your husband received the best of care. Dr. Ross is an excellent surgeon." He glanced at Dr. Ross. A flicker of skepticism entered her eyes. She must be wondering what he was up to. He'd meant what he'd said about her skills. Her abilities exceeded many he'd shared an OR with but praise appeared to make her uncomfortable.

"I'm sorry that this could only be a short visit," Dr. Ross said to the woman. "After shift change you may stay longer. Why don't you have dinner and then come back to visit?"

"We will. Come on, kids. Thanks, Dr. Ross. Dr. Smith, nice to meet you."

He nodded as the family passed him on their way to the door.

Dr. Ross moved to where the nurse stood and began discussing the patient.

Ty silently stepped away. Based on the conversation he and Dr. Ross had had after the surgery, she probably hadn't appreciated him coming over to meet the family. There had been a couple of seconds there when he'd seen past her cold exterior to some emotion he couldn't give a name to.

Minutes after leaving the CICU Michelle knocked on the chief of surgery's office door.

"Enter," she heard from the other side of the door.

She didn't always agree with Dr. Marshall's decisions or directives but she did think he was fair. He had been a mentor of sorts to her and more than once had gone to bat for her when there had been a problem between her and Administration. For the most part, though, he left her alone to do her job. He was old school but supportive. When he'd gone through medical school it had been almost entirely a man's profession so a female heart surgeon had made him feel a little uneasy.

She opened the door, stepped in and closed it behind her. The balding doctor leaned back in his chair, interest written on his face.

"To what do I owe this visit? I don't think you've been in my office for some time."

"Bob, you know I don't complain much."

He nodded, his eyes intently watching her.

"But I can't allow the new supply anesthesiologist to work in my OR again."

Dr. Marshall propped his arms on his desk, concern on his face. "Is the patient okay?"

"The patient is fine. Doing very well really."

He relaxed. "Then what's the problem? Smith, I think his name is, came highly recommended. Good CV. Excellent, actually."

"I cannot have the man showing up late for procedures."

Bob looked at her incredulously. "Why did he show up late?"

"I don't know. He didn't say."

"Did you ask him?"

"No. I didn't. I just need the people on my team to be on time."

"If that is the only fault you can find I think you should ask him why. I know you run a tight ship but we are all late sometimes."

"I'm not."

Bob released an exaggerated huff. "I know you're not. It might be good if you were occasionally." He said the last few words so quietly that she almost missed them. "Michelle, I think you're overreacting a bit. We're short an anesthesiologist and I can't shift everyone around just to suit you. Smith is more than qualified in cardiothoracic surgery. Unless he has or is doing something to harm a patient, you're just going to have to find a way to work with him."

"But—"

"Michelle, I know you're a driven physician. I can appreciate that but I think you can work this out without involving me. Smith is only here for six weeks. Surely you can handle working with him that long."

His desk phone rang and his hand hovered over the receiver. "Let me know if there's an issue involving a patient." He picked up the phone and said, "Hello?"

She'd been dismissed. Opening the door, Michelle stepped out into the hall and closed it behind her.

With no support, she was left no choice but to get along with the new guy. How was she going to manage that? Everything about him rubbed her the wrong way.

Ty stepped out into the warm, damp May evening, glad to head home or at least to the place he'd call home for the next few weeks. He'd never known a real brick-and-mortar house until he'd been sixteen and had left his mother and father to go and live with his grandparents.

He shoved a hand through his hair and rolled his neck one way and then the other to get the kinks out. It had taken him longer than he'd anticipated but he'd finished introducing himself to the next day's OR patients before he'd left the hospital.

Hooking his black leather bomber jacket on his index finger, he slung it over his shoulder and started in the direction of his motorcycle. A woman dressed in what he could see was a trim-fitting skirt was walking some distance ahead.

In the dim light he couldn't make out the color of her hair or clothes but as a red-blooded man he couldn't help but notice the provocative sway of her hips as she walked in and out of the shadows. She moved as if she was a model strutting on a runway in Paris. It was a sexy stride if he'd ever seen one. He wouldn't mind making the woman's acquaintance while he was here. Maybe she worked in one of the business departments in the hospital. He'd have to make a few inquiries in the morning.

With a feeling of disappointment he watched her step

between two parked cars, leaving only her head visible. A minute later Ty approached the back of what must be her car. She glanced at him. The male anticipation he'd developed and fostered while watching her walk suddenly received an icy shower.

"Dr. Ross!" He couldn't have contained his astonishment if he'd tried. That amazingly hot strut belonged to the ice queen.

Her eyes widened in disbelief. The key fob she held fell to the ground.

"Dr. Smith. Are you looking for me?" Her voice sounded a little high.

He'd certainly been looking *at* her, admiring her even.

She kneeled gracefully to retrieve her keys. "Is something wrong with our patient?"

"As far as I know, the patient is fine."

"Then why are you here?"

"This is a public parking lot. My bike is just over there." He pointed past her.

She glanced over her shoulder in the direction he indicated. "You ride a motorcycle?" Her voice was both shocked and accusatory. "They're so dangerous."

"Ever been on one?"

"No!"

"Try it. You might like it."

He looked down at her trim ankles balanced on spiky high heels. "Of course, that outfit might draw attention if you did. You'd show so much thigh that you might be stopped for being a traffic hazard." He chuckled.

His grin grew when her head dipped in what could only be described as embarrassment. Unless he was mistaken, her cheeks were the same rosy pink he remembered her shoes as being. Something about her reaction made him believe that she wasn't used to receiving compliments from men. That barbed-wire attitude of hers probably kept her from getting many. She was certainly attractive enough to receive them.

"I have no interest in being a traffic hazard." She opened the door of the car, slid in and slammed the door between them.

She might not want to be one but the woman certainly had everything required.

Ty moved on through the lot. It was necessary for her to pass him to leave. As she drove by her gaze found his and held for a second of awareness before she sped up and was gone.

Yes, the next few weeks would unquestionably be interesting.

Michelle pulled into the drive of her mother's simple red-brick suburban home. It was located in a neighborhood where all the houses along the street looked similar. The curtains of the living-room window fluttered and her mother's face appeared. Getting out of the car, Michelle opened the back passenger door and removed two plastic bags of groceries.

She headed for the front door. Seconds before she reached it the door opened. "Mom, you didn't need to get up. I could have let myself in."

Her tall but frail-looking mother, with a dusting of gray in her hair, smiled. "I know, dear, but you have your hands full."

"And the doctor said to take it easy for a while."

"I have been. You worry too much. What do doctors know anyway?" Her smile grew.

Michelle returned her grin. It was a running joke between them. Her mother was very proud of Michelle and told her so often. As the only parent Michelle had left, she worried about her mother, unable to stand the thought of losing her in both body and spirit. Then she would be alone in the world.

"Mom, why don't you come and sit in the kitchen while I put these groceries away and see about getting us some supper?"

"I'd like that. You can tell me about your day. You work too hard, you know. Doing surgery all day and then coming here to see about me."

That was also a continuing argument between them. One that neither one of them seemed to ever win.

Her mother followed Michelle along the familiar hallway to the small but cozy kitchen. This was Michelle's favorite room in the house. It was where she remembered her father best. Even years after his death she and her mother still didn't sit in what was considered "his chair".

As Michelle prepared the simple meal, her mother chatted about the book she was reading and the neighborhood children who had stopped by to sell her cookies. Michelle felt bad that her mother had to spend so much time alone. She'd been such an active woman until the cancer had been discovered. Her recovery was coming along well but Michelle worried that her mother had lost hope. Worse, Michelle feared *she* might have. She fixed hearts. Cancer wasn't her department. She had no control here and she was having a difficult time dealing with that fact.

With all those years of medical school and all her surgical skills, she was no more capable of saving her mother than the guy down at the gas station. Cancer had a way of leveling the playing field. No one was more likely to live than another. The only thing anyone really shared was hope. That knowledge not only made her angry but it made her feel desperate.

Michelle placed a plate in front of her mother and another at her own lifelong place. Filling their glasses with iced tea, she set them on the table and took her chair.

"So, how was your day? Anything special happen?" her mother asked, as she poked at the roast chicken in front of her.

Suddenly the broad-shouldered, unorthodox anesthesiologist with the dark unruly hair flashed into her mind. Of all the people to be the highlight of her day.

"No, nothing special. My surgery cases went well, which always makes it a good day."

"You know you really should go out some."

Michelle let out an exasperated breath. She changed lives through surgery for the better almost daily and some days saved a life that would soon be lost. Despite that, her mother was still only interested in her dating. No matter how old or successful she became, her mother wanted her to find someone special.

Michelle wasn't against the idea. The right person just hadn't come along. She had to admit that it would be nice to have a man in her life. A serious man who could understand her. It would be wonderful to have a marriage like her mom and dad's had been.

"Michelle, you have no fun in your life. You worked too hard. When you're not at the hospital you spend your evenings here, visiting me. You need to live a little."

This had become an almost daily conversation. "Mom, I love spending time with you."

"Aren't there any young men working at that hospital you might like?"

The aggravating anesthesiologist's twinkling eyes popped into her mind. "None that I'd ever be interested in."

Ty opened the door to the nondescript furnished apartment. His surroundings didn't bother him. After years of living in other spaces like it, he was more than used to this type of place. At least there would be a roof over his head, which was more than he could say about his childhood.

Pushing the large brown box with his name on it inside with his foot, he closed the door behind him. A cardboard box had become his suitcase of choice. His guitar should be delivered tomorrow. He'd arranged to have it shipped to the hospital so that someone would be around to sign for it and put it in a safe place. Sometimes he traveled with it on the bike but he didn't like to. It was one of the few things he'd taken with him when he'd left his parents.

He dropped his helmet on the chair closest to the door and headed for the kitchen. He placed the sack holding the package of gourmet coffee on the counter then looked for the coffeemaker. Great. The machine was a good one. It had been his only request.

Doctors to Go, the service he worked for and was a fifty percent owner of, had seen that he had one. Ty had been working for the company a year when his friend had offered Ty part of the business. Owning nothing but a motorcycle and the clothes on his back, he'd saved his paychecks. There had also been the small amount he'd inherited when his grandfather had died, so he'd had the funds to invest.

His partner ran the show and Ty stayed in the background as a very silent partner. No boardrooms or conference calls for him. One of the ideals that his grandfather had drummed into him early after he moved in with his grandparents had been to plan for the future. Something his parents would have never considered. He'd done as his grandfather had suggested, but he loved working with people so he still continued to practice medicine.

He didn't generally frequent grocery stores when he moved to a new city. Instead, he chose to take most of his meals at the hospital. Otherwise he asked around about local mom-and-pop places that served good down-home cooking. Ty had already been given a few names of places from a couple of the surgery team members. He'd try one of the restaurants on his day off.

Ty prepared and set the coffeemaker to start percolating at five a.m., before he headed for the shower. Stripping off and turning the water on, he stepped under the shower head. Not all the places he'd stayed had had great showers but having one available was more than he'd had growing up. Rain barrels and creeks just didn't compare to a hot spray with excellent water pressure.

A muffled ring came from the clothes he'd dropped on the floor. He pushed the shower curtain back, picked up his discarded jeans and dug into the pocket for his phone. His partner had texted earlier that he would be calling about an issue with the business.

"Smith here. Let me call you right back. I'm in the shower."

"Uh, Dr. Smith. It's Dr. Ross," came a soft, stilted voice.

"Who?"

"Dr. Ross." Emphasis and impatience surrounded the enunciation of the name.

"Oh, Michelle. I thought you were someone else."

"Obviously."

He could just see her nose turning up as she said the word. The woman was far too stuffy. "How can I help you, Michelle?" He did like the sound of her name. It suited her.

"Our case has been moved up to first thing in the morning."

He held the phone with two fingers to keep water from running over it. "I thought that the anesthesia department clerk made these calls."

"Normally she does, but I was called and couldn't get her, so I'm calling."

If nothing else, she was thorough. He couldn't fault that. It no doubt made her a good doctor. "How did you get my number?"

"I make it a point to have the numbers of everyone on my team."

"I see." He let the words drag out for emphasis. "You have it for no other reason?"

"No. There is no other. I'll see you at seven sharp."

He chuckled at her haughty tone. It sounded as if she were saying the words through a clenched jaw. He couldn't help taunting her. She seemed like the kind of person who always rose to the bait. If only he could see her face.

"I'll be there. Now, if you don't mind I'll finish my shower."

"Oh. Uh…sure. Bye."

So the frosty woman could be rattled. Stepping back into the shower, he thought he might have to do that more often. But what had him giving the stiff, buttoned-up woman even a second thought? She certainly wasn't his type. Everything about her screamed of stability.

He'd been accused on more than one occasion of being the love-them-and-leave-them type. No woman got promises or commitments from him. That way he didn't hurt them. Others could plant roots but they weren't for him.

There had been a couple of women he'd dated who had made noises about him settling down. When that had happened it hadn't taken him long until he'd been on his way to the next hospital in the next town. He wasn't the type of person someone should depend on. When the going got tough he'd only let them down.

He liked women who enjoyed life, laughed, had fun and that was all they were interested in from the relationship. Michelle seemed far too serious about everything. She didn't strike him as a short but enjoyable affair type of woman, even if he had been interested in having one with her. Which he wasn't.

Enough about her. He needed some rest, especially if he was going to have to face her early in the morning and be on his best behavior. Which he wasn't sure he could do.

He turned off the water and stepped out of the shower. Snatching a towel off the rack, he dried off. Thank goodness he'd requested maid service to start yesterday. Minutes later, naked, he slipped between cool sheets.

Dr. Ross's strut across the parking lot came to mind. His weeks in Raleigh might be far more fascinating than he'd anticipated.

CHAPTER TWO

EARLY THE NEXT morning, Michelle tapped lightly on the door of her first case for the day.

Shawn Russell. Twenty years old. His procedure would be difficult. As a congenital heart patient he'd grown up in the hospital system and would never really leave it. Shawn was quite unhappy with the prospect of having surgery again. This time he needed to have the heart valve he'd outgrown replaced. Not a demanding surgery in most patients but in those with multiple surgeries the development of scar tissue added a degree of difficulty.

At the sound of "Come in", Michelle pushed the door open further. The room was filled with people, undoubtedly family and friends. Dr. Smith stood beside Shawn's bed with his back to her. Having only known him a day, she still recognized his dark hair and broad back.

He glanced around. "Good morning, Dr. Ross. We were just talking about you," he said with a grin.

Michelle raised an uncertain brow. Never a fan of people discussing her, she wasn't sure she was happy with what Dr. Smith might have been saying.

More than once she'd heard the whispers after she'd gone by the nurses' desk. But instead of those negative thoughts his grin brought back memories of their conversation the evening before when he'd announced unabashedly that he was in the shower. He'd been trying to get a reaction out of her. She planned to see he didn't get one.

"I was checking on Shawn to see if he had any questions for me before he goes into the OR," Dr. Smith offered.

She nodded. "Good."

Dr. Smith pushed his dark hair back away from his face. There was nothing conservative about its length or cut. Worn long and being wavy and thick, it curled behind his ears. It was the kind of hair that women envied. He certainly didn't meet what she considered the standard dress code.

"Did you know that Shawn is a master gamer?"

What was he talking about? "No, I didn't. That's great." She looked at Shawn. "Do you have any questions about the surgery?"

The far-too-thin young man shook his head. "I think my mother does."

"I'll go and let Dr. Ross speak to your parents. I'll see you in the OR in a few minutes. The nurse will give you something to make you happy." Dr. Smith grinned. "Don't get too used to it because you don't get to carry any of it home." He put out his fist and Shawn butted his against it. "Later, man. Remember you promised me a game."

"Sure, Dr. Smith."

"Make it Ty, man. See you soon."

Shawn nodded and gave him a small smile. For the first time since she'd met Shawn he didn't look terrified. She and Dr. Smith might have gotten off on the wrong foot but she had to give him kudos for making patients feel comfortable. She would like to be that easy with people but it wasn't her strong suit.

Half an hour later Michelle entered the OR prep area. Dr. Smith stood at the scrub sink along with three of the OR nurses. The group was chattering non-stop. Dr. Smith seemed to be the ringleader, interjecting a random comment which would bring on a burst of laughter from the women around him.

For the first time Michelle felt like an outsider. She couldn't remember ever feeling that way so intensely before, or caring. She had no idea how to join their conversation. Worse, she couldn't understand why all of a sudden she wanted to. What would it be like to belong? To know what was happening in the staff's lives, for them to know what was happening in hers? Could she ever have that type of relationship with her coworkers? With anyone?

She remembered having friends over to spend the night as a kid. After her father had died that had become less frequent. She'd found out pretty quickly that her friends hadn't felt comfortable with her any longer. The sadness she'd felt over the loss of her beloved father had been far too much for them. She'd started spending more and more time at home, reading and studying. It had been easier than trying to pretend to be having a good time with people who didn't understand.

Her father was gone and her friends had slowly left also.

Michelle's mother had encouraged her to go out to football games, to the prom, but to Michelle all those things had seemed silly. She'd also hated to leave her mother alone. They'd become a team. As the years had gone by Michelle had lost most of her small-talk skills, choosing to focus on medicine instead of a social life. Her mother, school and then her job had taken all her time, leaving little to devote to building outside relationships. There had been a few men who had shown her attention. Most had only been interested in her for her looks. Few had appreciated her intellect. They hadn't stayed around long.

A second later another nurse joined the group. Dr. Smith did have a way of drawing not only women to him but men as well. People liked him. She had to admit she was as aware of the man as the rest of them. She just refused to let it show, had more command over her reactions.

Unable to wait any longer to scrub in so that she could begin her procedure on time, she stepped towards the sink when a spot became available. Just as she took her place, the group erupted in laughter.

Dr. Smith turned, almost bumping into her. "Hey, Michelle."

Out of the corner of her eye she noticed the other women drifting away. She placed a foot on the pedal to start the water. "Hi," she said, concentrating on washing.

"We were just talking about getting together tonight at a bar downtown. I've been asked to fill in as part of the surgeons' band."

"You play?"

"Don't sound so surprised. I play a mean guitar. I think that's why Schwartz requested me to take his place. More for my guitar skills than my medical ones."

"I didn't know Dr. Schwartz played in the band."

Had he said he wasn't surprised? She refused to let him make her feel like she didn't belong. "No, it doesn't surprise me that you play guitar. I was just making conversation."

"Interesting. You don't strike me as someone who makes small talk." Was he trying to needle her on purpose?

"I don't believe you know me well enough to know what I do."

He pressed his lips together and nodded as if in deep thought. "You're right. Maybe we should try to change that."

Michelle looked at him. Where was this going?

"A group of us are getting together after the band plays on Saturday night. Why don't you join us then? Practice that small talk."

"I'm busy."

"Well, if your plans change we're going to be at Buster's. Wherever that is."

"It's right in the central part of the old city."

"A surgeon and a tour guide. Two for one," he said with a grin.

She smirked at him. "My father used to take me there for burgers when I was a kid." Why was she telling him this?

"Really, your father took you to a bar?" His tone implied he was teasing.

She made an exasperated noise. "My father would never have taken me to a bar."

Dr. Smith chuckled. The man was baiting her again. Wasn't he ever serious?

"It wasn't a bar then. Just a grill. Mr. Roberts owned the place and was a friend of my father's. I don't know what it's like now, but it was once a place with brick walls and had these old wooden tables."

"You haven't been lately?"

"Not since I was a child."

"Why not?"

"I just hadn't thought about going." That wasn't true. It had been her and her father's special place. The memories were just too strong there. They made her miss her father more.

"Maybe it's time to try it again."

She finished scrubbing her nails. "I don't think so."

"Well, I hope you change your mind. It could be fun. If they still have burgers, I'll buy you one," he said, passing her on his way toward the OR.

A few minutes later she entered behind him. The team was talking and softly laughing at something Ty must have said. He seemed to always be saying something outrageous. She couldn't blame her team for reacting. She'd smiled more since she'd met him than she had in a long time, but her nerves had been on edge just as often.

Everyone quieted down and became attentive when she joined them. "Are we ready to begin? By the way, it's nice to see you here ahead of me, Dr. Smith." Her voice carried a teasing tone. She didn't tease. What was happening to her?

"Glad to be here. This time I wasn't stuck helping out at a car accident." His gaze caught and held hers.

He'd made his point. It figured he'd have a good reason that would make her feel bad about her actions the day before. "Understandable. I hope everyone was okay."

"Everyone was fine. I'm ready to begin when you are, Michelle." His eyes twinkled when he said her name.

Her jaw tightened beneath her mask. Demanding that the aggravating man call her by her formal name in the OR was a battle she didn't think she could win. She'd let it go unless it happened at an improper time, like in front of a patient.

She glanced around to find all eyes on her. Their faces were covered but she had a sense that their mouths had dropped open. She imagined they were following the interaction between her and Ty with great interest.

Unwilling to let the team know he'd gotten a reaction out of her, she cleared her throat and said in her most efficient tone, "Let's begin."

Later, Ty sat behind the nurses' station on the heart floor, reviewing patient charts before his pre-op visits. He and Michelle would share three cases the next day. Finished with the chart he'd been reviewing, he closed it as the clip-clip of heels tapping tiles drew his attention. He looked up to see Michelle coming towards him. Her hair was pulled tight behind her head and she was dressed in soft gray pants with a silky pale pink blouse. Over that she wore a finely pressed lab jacket. There wasn't a wrinkle on it and he'd bet a weeks' pay it was starched. Her high heels were the same dove-gray as her pants except for the tips of the toes, which were hot pink.

Disappointment filled him over missing a view of her legs. She had exceptionally fine legs.

For such a strong-willed woman she sure wore feminine colors. This outfit was just as tailored as yesterday's, letting no one mistake her as anything other than a female. She was a paradox. All hard edges in manner and all soft and sensual curves in looks. Which was the truer Michelle? He'd like to know.

She glanced in his direction. When he smiled she quickly looked away and continued towards the room of one of her cases. He returned his attention to the computer screen and the chart of his next patient.

Opening another file, he looked up to see the nurse assigned to Shawn stamping toward the desk. Her lips were clamped into a tight, thin line. She stopped in front of the nurse sitting two chairs down from him. Through clenched teeth she hissed, "Abby, please watch my patient for a few minutes. The ice queen is riding her broom again."

The nurse she spoke to looked none too happy but she said, "Okay. But don't be long. I don't want to be in her line of fire either."

"I just need to blow off some steam for a minute. At least she has moved on to poor Robin's patient."

Ty saw Michelle approaching, but the two nurses had not. He didn't miss the look of glass-shard pain in Michelle's eyes before she blinked and her face became an unemotional mask. He had no doubt she'd heard every word. It had hurt her. By the look in her eyes—deeply.

"Excuse me, if you are not too busy, could you get me a number where I can reach Shawn's family?"

The first nurse wheeled about, shock covering her face. "Uh, yes, yes, ma'am. I have it in the chart."

The nurse must have forgotten about blowing off steam because she hurried to pull up the chart on one of the computers behind the desk.

Ty focused his attention on Michelle but she didn't even glance at him.

The nurse handed a slip of paper to Michelle.

"Thank you," she said stiffly.

She walked off. For once Ty felt sorry for her.

Not long afterwards, Ty started his pre-op rounds, visiting the patients on the next day's surgery schedule. One of them was running a fever. He'd have to speak to Michelle about postponing surgery at least a day.

He could call her but after what had happened earlier he felt compelled to talk to her personally. Just for a second when she'd turned to leave he'd seen a crack in her mask, a deep sadness. He asked a nurse where to find her office. While he walked down the long hall in that direction, he told himself that he would be concerned about anyone who might have had their feelings hurt so publicly. It had nothing to do with Michelle in particular. He made a point not to get involved on a personal level. So why had her reaction gotten to him?

Stopping at the woodgrained door with her name on a plate beside it, he tapped. Seconds later a subdued, "Come in," reached his ears.

Opening the door, he stepped in. The blast of color before him made him jolt to a stop. The walls of Michelle's office were a warm yellow but what really got his attention was the huge bright red poppy painting hanging behind Michelle's head. That, he hadn't expected. The woman just got more interesting all the time. Her desk was the traditional hospital style but on it were modern office supplies, not typical business issue. There were two bright ultra-modern chairs covered in a fabric that coordinated with the painting and the color of the walls in front of her desk. This was obviously her haven.

Michelle's eyes widened when she saw him. They were bloodshot, pink-rimmed. His gut squeezed. She'd been crying. She wouldn't be happy he'd noticed either. He moved toward her desk.

"What can I help you with, Dr. Smith?" Her flat tone said she wanted to get rid of him as quickly as possible.

"Please make it Ty."

With a sound of annoyance she said, "Is there a problem…Ty?"

Michelle said his name as if it was painful. She still resisted any relationship that being on a first-name basis implied.

"Mr. Marcus has spiked a fever." He glanced down at the garbage can sitting beside her desk. Inside were Cellophane wrappers and white paper squares. She'd been eating chocolate cake rolls, no doubt feeding her emotions. So the woman was undeniably human.

When his gaze came back up it was seconds before hers met his. It quickly fluttered away again.

"I'm sorry you overheard them." He didn't take his eyes off her.

She didn't question to what he referred. Instead, she sat straighter and said, "We need to start Mr. Marcus on prophylactic antibiotics and postpone his surgery until the day after tomorrow."

"I agree."

"Is there anything further?" Michelle shifted some papers on her desk that he suspected she really hadn't been working on. She was trying to get him to leave without coming out and saying it. Still, he couldn't bring himself to just forget that she'd been crying before he'd entered the office. Despite her less than warm demeanor toward him, he wanted to help her. He wanted to peel away the layers and find out what made the woman tick.

"I can *see* that you've already had dessert but I was wondering if you might like to grab a meal with me. I heard there is a place not far from here that serves a great roast-beef platter."

She looked up at him as if he had snakes in his hair. "No, thank you. I have work to do."

"Then maybe another time."

"I don't think so."

He leaned his hip against her desk and looked down at where she sat. She glared at him pointedly.

"What sticks in your craw about me? Or is it you can't stand anyone?" He raised a hand to stop her from interrupting. "It's none of my business, and you can pretend differently, but I know your feelings were hurt a while ago. All you have to do is show them that you're human. Smile, ask about their families. Win them over a little."

Michelle stood with a jerk. Placing both hands on the edge of her desk, she leaned towards him. "You think I don't know what the staff thinks about me? It isn't my job to be friends with them. My patients' care comes first and foremost. How dare you come in and try to tell me how to run my life? I don't need some flit-in and flit-out doctor to tell me how I need to interact with the nurses."

A slow grinned came to his lips. He'd expected her righteous indignation. "I'm just saying you can catch more flies with honey than you can with vinegar."

She sputtered her disgust as he turned to leave.

At two in the morning Michelle pushed open the door of the physicians' entrance to the hospital and stepped out into the night. Her team had been called in to handle an emergency. Thankfully she didn't do too much surgery in the early hours of the morning. A hospital took on an other-world feeling late at night. Spooky yet peaceful.

She was so tired she hadn't bothered to change out of her scrubs. Something that rarely happened. Her hair was still pulled back and secured by a rubber band, producing a small ponytail that brushed her neck. Holding her small purse in her hand, she was taking her first step towards her car when the door behind her opened. She jumped. Glancing back, she saw Ty. In one way it was a relief that it wasn't someone with nefarious ideas; in another he wasn't her favorite person.

This was the first time outside the OR she'd seen him since their conversation, turned blow-out on her part, hours earlier. She had cooled off but she still didn't know why he thought he had the right to offer her advice. Especially the unsolicited kind.

She started walking.

"Nice work in there, Michelle," he called.

She stopped and looked back at him. The lighting in the parking area wasn't dim enough to disguise his drained stance. For once he wasn't being upbeat and bubbly. He seemed as tired as she was. He'd changed out of his scrubs and now wore a light-colored T-shirt that fit his muscular shoulders far too tightly for her not to notice. A pair of baggy cargo shorts and sandals finished off his outfit.

On anyone else those clothes might have looked like those of a bum, but on Ty they added to his bad-boy sex appeal. His hair was no longer tied back, like he'd worn it under his surgery cap. Instead, it looked as if he'd pushed his hands through it and let it go. He looked untamed and wild.

"Whew, this early-morning stuff isn't as easy as it used

to be in med school. Who I'm I trying to kid? It wasn't easy then." He came to stand beside her.

Did he think that she was going to act as if nothing had happened between them? "No, it wasn't." She started walking again.

"Michelle, wait."

She stopped and turned again. "Why? So you can tell me what I need to do?"

"Ooh, so the woman can carry a grudge."

"I'm not carrying a grudge! I just don't like people butting into my business."

"Maybe you just don't like people," he said in an even tone.

She stepped toward him. "I do like people."

"Then prove it."

"Prove it?" What was he talking about?

"Yeah. Say one nice thing about me."

She let out a dry chuckle.

He tilted his head and studied her. "You know, I think that's the first time I've heard you approach anything near a laugh."

"I laugh."

"When? When no one is around?" he asked, moving passed her.

"Are you trying to start an argument?"

He paused this time. "No, I was trying to give you a compliment. Maybe flirt with you a little."

"I don't want you flirting with me."

"Why not?"

She pinned him with a look. Even in the faint light she could see his wicked grin. She had no doubt that his eyes were twinkling. "Because nothing about you says you're serious about anything."

"That's not true. I'm always serious about caring for my patients."

"You know what I mean. All the nurses flock to you. I've even seen women from different departments come to the floor who have never been there before to see or hopefully be seen by Ty Smith."

"Hey, you can't fault me for that."

He was right, but she wasn't becoming one of his groupies. "Why don't you make their day by flirting with them and leave me alone?"

"Because you doth protest too much. You're far too much fun to tease. I can always count on a pretty blush and a sharp rebuttal. You challenge my mind."

"Humph." She started walking toward her car. "So you've decided I'm going to be your entertainment while you're in town. I'm not flattered."

He fell into step beside her. "The way you say it doesn't make it sound too nice. Like I'm pulling wings off butterflies. Has it ever occurred to you that I might be attracted to you?"

"No."

"No." He voice held total disbelief. "You don't think I could be attracted to you or, no, you don't think I'm attracted to you?"

"Both."

"My, you're mighty cynical for such a beautiful and intelligent woman."

She put her hands on her hips and really looked at him. "Ty, I'm no one's good-time girl. I already have enough worries, without adding you to my list."

"Don't you ever just want to have a good time?"

"I don't have time for a good time." She clicked the fob to unlock her car then opened the door.

"Hey, you never said what you like about me."

She slipped under the wheel. "Goodnight, Ty." And closed the door.

Looking into the rear-view window, she saw him saunter over to where a motorcycle was parked. He had a loose-hipped walk that belied his size. Letting him get into her head wasn't a good idea.

She stuck her key into the ignition and turned it. A clicking noise was all that happened. She tried it again. The engine refused to start.

The zoom of a motorcycle being turned off made her look into the mirror. Ty was getting off his bike and putting the kickstand down. She opened the car door. "The battery is dead."

He stepped closer. "You've had trouble with it before?"

"Yeah. It was a little slow to start when I headed here. I was going to have it seen to tomorrow."

"Well, it looks like you're going to need a ride home."

She searched for her phone. "I'll call a taxi."

"I'll give you a lift."

"I don't think so. I'll just wait here for a taxi."

"Be realistic, Michelle. How long do you think it will take for a taxi to show up at this hour? And you're sure as heck not going to sit in a dark parking lot and wait."

"I can go inside."

"Come on. Let me give you a drive home. I'll ride slowly. No fancy moves."

Still unsure, she was exhausted and the thought of having to wait another hour or longer to head home wasn't appealing. She grabbed her purse as she climbed out of the car. "Okay, but no nonsense. I saw one too many motorcycle victims when I was doing my ER rotation."

"I promise, only one wheelie."

"What?" She stepped back, planning to refuse to get on.
"Kidding. Just kidding."

Ty was pleased he hadn't had to do a more convincing
job of selling Michelle on the idea of riding on his bike.
Most women he'd known had seemed to be fascinated by
the prospect. It was part of his mystique. For him, it was
cheap and easy transportation. Apparently Michelle wasn't
impressed one way or another with his air of mystery. For
some reason he wished she was, but was glad she wasn't.
He never dipped below the surface of his emotions and he
didn't want anyone else to do it either.

He unlocked the seat compartment, pulled out a spare
helmet and offered it to her. His hand remained suspended
in mid-air for a moment before she took it. She made no
further movement.

"You do know that you have to put it on to ride? It's
the law."

She look around as if there might be a state trooper
watching.

He shoved his hair back, preparing to slip on his own
helmet. Michelle remained rooted to the spot as if she
couldn't make up her mind whether or not this was a good
idea. "Are you coming or not?" Again she scanned the parking lot like she was hoping for any other option. Taking a
deep breath, she put the helmet on her head. It wouldn't go
into place because of her hair.

"Here, let me help you." He lifted the helmet off her
head and reached around to release her hair. He could feel
her breath on his neck.

She bent her torso away from him. "What're you doing?"

"Trying to get your head into this helmet. Your hair is
stopping it from going on."

"Oh."

"What did you think I was doing? Making a play for you?"

"No."

"Yes, you did." He looked her straight in the eyes, wishing the streetlights were brighter. "If and when I make a play for you, you won't need to question what I'm doing. It will be perfectly clear." With great satisfaction he watched her throat bob up and down. "Now I'm tired and I'm hungry. If you would like me to take you home you're going to have to let me help you with the helmet. Of course, I can also escort you to the lobby so you can wait for a taxi there. Either way, I'd like to get a move on."

She pulled the rubber band out of her hair and plopped the helmet down on her head.

So the ice queen responded to authority.

"I'm going to fix the chin strap now," he said in an exaggerated voice, as if speaking to a child.

"Stop making fun of me. I've never been on a motorcycle before."

She gave him such a pointed look of defiance that he wanted to take off the helmet and kiss her.

"I'm still not sure you're the one I want to take my first ride with."

He chuckled as he picked up his helmet from the handlebars. "I promise it will be a ride to remember." After slipping on his helmet, he said, "Hand me your purse. I'll put it under the seat."

Michelle did so, after only a moment of hesitation. Storing the purse and closing the seat, he then threw a leg over the bike, pushed the kickstand up and revved the engine. The bike roared to life. He looked back over his shoulder. "By the definition of ride, you have to get on first."

She lifted a leg over the seat. He had the sense that she was making every effort not to touch him. When she tottered, a hand gripped his shoulder then was gone, only to return just as quickly. He'd watched those long, delicate fingers do meticulous surgery. Now he felt their strength. What would it be like to have her want to touch him all over?

She pulled her hands away again as she settled on the bike.

"You need to move up close and hang on or you'll fall off the back."

Michelle shifted closer but acted as if she was making sure her legs didn't touch his. She held a fistful of shirt in each hand, instead of wrapping her hands around his waist.

"Ready?"

She nodded.

"Okay. Here we go." He clicked the bike into gear, let off the hand clutch and the bike moved across the lot. Less than five seconds later Michelle's arms had his waist in a death grip. Her thighs squeezed his where they met, and her face and chest were plastered to his back.

His manhood rose in response. He sucked in a breath. This had been such a bad idea on so many levels. The woman was terrified and he was turned on.

He took his hand off the handlebars long enough to pat her knee. "You're doing great."

As he turned right out of the parking lot, he realized he had no idea where she lived. He'd spent so much time trying to convince her to get on the bike that he'd forgotten to ask for directions. "Which way is your house?" he called over his shoulder.

There was no answer.

"Point in the direction I need to go."

Again he heard nothing.

"Michelle, we can't just drive around all night. You have to tell me where you live."

She lifted one finger against his stomach and pointed ahead.

"I'm going the right way?"

She nodded against his back.

It was far too late for word games. He needed directions and she seemed incapable of giving them. Just up the street was the bright sign of an all-night diner. He was hungry and because they had done surgery tonight they wouldn't be required to be at the hospital until the day after tomorrow. They had time to stop.

He pulled into the parking lot and under the glaring lights. As he eased the bike to a stop, Michelle's grip on him slackened. He missed her warm, soft breasts pressed tightly against him. As if she realized she was still holding onto him, her arms fell away and she pushed back on the seat.

"What're we doing here?"

"Getting some breakfast."

"I want to go home."

"In that case, you're going to have to tell me how to get there. Which you couldn't do on the bike. So while you give me directions, I'm going to get some eggs and bacon. Care to join me?"

Once again she looked unsure. It always caught him by surprise because she was so formidable in the OR. Maybe the overconfident woman wasn't so self-assured after all.

"I am kind of hungry."

She put one foot on the ground and grabbed his shoulder as she brought the other over. He climbed off. Michelle was already in the process of removing her helmet. When she got it off he took it from her and laid it beside his on the seat.

The diner looked like it had been around forever. It was a fifties-type place with silver siding, orange bench seats, and Formica tabletops. He loved the place already.

He held the door open for Michelle. Her hair was mussed and she still wore green scrubs but that didn't detract from her stately walk or good looks. She could have been a conquering queen by the way she held herself. What made her even more eye-catching was that it was a natural part of who she was, nothing conceited about it.

There were only a handful of people in the place but all eyes turned to her. She ignored them and scooted into the first booth she came to. Ty moved in across from her.

"I thought you might like to sit where you can see your bike."

"Good plan."

"How long have you been riding?" she asked as she picked up a plastic-covered menu.

"Since I was about sixteen."

"That young?" Her eyes widened.

"Yeah. I had to have a way to get to and from school."

She looked up over the menu. "Your parents let you have a motorcycle at that age?"

"No, my grandfather did." Whoa, she'd already gotten more personal information out of him than most people did. Usually he steered the conversation away from himself but Michelle wasn't giving him a chance to as she shot off another question.

"How did your parents feel about that?"

"They didn't care."

She looked down at the double-sided card in her hand and mumbled, "I sure would have."

"They weren't around to care." Bitterness filled his voice but, then, it always did when he spoke about his parents. Which he rarely did.

Thankfully the server approached their table. She was in her mid-forties, slightly overweight and had her thin hair tied back in a ponytail. "What you have?"

"Hi, there. I'll have the breakfast platter. Eggs over easy."

When the woman looked at her, Michelle said, "And I'd like the mile-high pancakes."

Ty smiled up at the server. "And a large pot of fresh coffee."

The woman smiled. "Coming up."

"You're amazing. That woman looked so sour when she came over to take our order and she leaves smiling because she has spoken to you."

"Why, thank you. Nothing but the power of Ty."

"The power of Ty, uh? Ty is a nickname, isn't it? I'd guess your full name is Tyrone."

Michelle was being unusually chatty. Maybe it was the late hour, maybe she was hungry or maybe it was the fact she was stuck with him. Normally he would have complained about all the personal questions but he found he didn't want to give her a reason to stop. It was good and bad. He liked her attention too much and she was uncovering his secrets.

"I was named after Tyrone, Georgia."

"Why after a town?'

"Because my parents were passing through it when my mother went into labor. You sure are full of questions."

"It's interesting. I've never known anyone named after a town. So you were born in Tyrone."

Ty hesitated a moment before he said more. He'd told maybe three other people about his birth. "No, I was born in a stand of trees beside a cotton field."

"What?"

"My parents didn't believe in going to the hospital." He put his fingers in the air to make quotation marks. "Birth is a natural process. You don't need a hospital for that."

"In this day and age I can't imagine that happening."

For Joey no doctor and no hospital, going all natural, had

been a death sentence. Ty had seen to it that he was no longer associated with those ideas. "Well, it didn't just happen yesterday. I am thirty-four years old." Okay, now he'd said enough. For someone who had a difficult time building relationships at work, Michelle sure had him spilling his guts.

"You know what I mean. Medicine has advanced so far. We know so much more than we used to."

"Yeah, science has come a long way but not everyone embraces it, neither does it have all the answers." That statement made it sound like he was defending his parents, which he certainly was not.

Michelle's eyes went dark and a sheen of moisture covered them before she blinked. What had she been thinking about to bring that on?

Her eyes rose to meet his. They held a stricken look for a second before her gaze focused downward. Had he stumbled on a secret? He didn't want to look into anyone's dark closet.

To his great relief, the server returned to place Michelle's plate down in front of her then his in front of him. Now he'd make an effort to turn the conversation to something less personal and certainly more pleasant.

"Whoo, comfort food. I might think you're feeding your emotions."

"I like pancakes. Nothing special there."

He was beginning to think there were a number of things special about Michelle.

"Still an amazing amount of food for such a shapely woman."

"Shapely?"

"Don't try to act like you don't know you're a fine-looking woman."

"Thank you," she said in a humble-sounding voice.

"How do you stay in such good shape?"

"I swim laps three times a week and I have good genes. My mother…"

She put a bit of pancake in her mouth but he had the feeling she had purposely decided not to say more.

"Interesting. I took you for a gym rat. But on second thoughts that would be far too sociable for you."

'That didn't sound like a compliment. More like an insult. You don't think I can be sociable?"

"I had no intention of insulting you." This subject was more like it. Less about him and superficial. "I was just stating fact from what I've seen. And, no, I don't think you are particularly sociable."

Her eyes drifted away to watch the server pour coffee. Michelle looked up at him again. "So how do you stay in shape?"

"So you think I look good?"

"That isn't what I said. My arms were around your body just a few minutes ago. I have some idea of your physical fitness."

He knew all too well how close she'd been. How much he'd enjoyed it. His body had taken far too long to recover from the contact. The ice queen was thawing. Nicely.

"I enjoy rock climbing, wind surfing when I'm stationed close enough to the ocean, and I try to pick up a game of basketball in the local park when I can."

"Sounds like you stay busy."

"I try to. Moving from town to town can be lonely so I try to get out where people are." He forked eggs into his mouth.

She gave him a long look he couldn't quite read.

"So how did you like your first bike ride?"

"I found it exhilarating."

His lowered his chin and pierced her with a look. "I

thought by the King Kong grip you had on my waist that you might be terrified."

"I was but that doesn't mean I wasn't enjoying it."

He nodded his head in fascination. "You're an intriguing woman, Dr. Ross."

"You never call me Dr. Ross."

"Yes, I do. In front of patients."

Michelle huffed. Which she did often, but he found that he liked it. "Why do you insist on calling me Michelle when you know I'd rather you didn't?"

"At first it was to aggravate you, then it was because 'Dr. Ross' sounds so stuffy in the OR and now it's because I like the feel of it crossing my lips."

Ty didn't miss her shiver or the fact that her fork came to rest a little too noisily against her plate. He'd pierced that armor she hid behind. The opposite of cold was hot. Maybe beneath that snowcap attitude was a boiling volcano of emotion ready to erupt. It would be exciting to be there when it did.

"I'd take that as praise but for the fact that the hospital Casanova said it."

"I'm no Casanova. I just consider myself a friendly person." He took a sip of his coffee.

"With all the women."

"Are you just a little jealous, Michelle?"

He made her name sound particularly sexy on purpose. Maybe he could light some fire under that snow. Her eyelids fluttered down and up again. Oh, yes, he was getting to her. But why did he want to? There were plenty of woman at the hospital who had made it clear on a number of occasions that they were more than charmed. But who did he find intriguing? Michelle.

That revelation made him sit back in his seat. He watched Michelle for a moment. She was certainly attractive enough but her standoffish ways were perturbing. He wanted to have fun and nothing about this woman said fun. That wasn't entirely true, he was having a good time right now. Still, Michelle was definitely the wrong person to be interested in. She cried permanence and that wasn't in his plans in any form.

"I am not jealous. Why would I be?"

He gave her a thoughtful look. "I don't know. Maybe because you want me for yourself?"

She glared at him. "Now you're making things up."

Minutes later she finished the last bit of pancake and took a slip of coffee. She leaned back in the booth and yawned.

"I'd better get you home to bed," Ty said, pulling out his wallet.

"Why Doctor, do you say that to every surgeon you work with?"

His heart skipped a beat. "Why, Doctor, are you flirting with me?"

Her eyes went wide and she squared her shoulders. "I've never flirted in my life."

Ty could believe that. "Well, there's always a first time for everything. And I do believe that you were."

"It won't happen again." Her serious tone returned.

"I sure hope that isn't true. I enjoyed it. Hey, before we go, draw me a map to your house."

"I live in a condo."

"Okay, condo."

"Ma'am," Michelle called to the server, "may I have a piece of paper and borrow a pen?"

She looked back at Ty. "I usually have a notepad with me."

"I'm not surprised."

"What does that mean?"

"It means you're always prepared." His tone implied he wasn't impressed by her thoroughness.

When the server didn't immediately fulfill her request, he picked up a napkin. "Here, just use this."

"A napkin?"

"Yeah, you've never written on a napkin?

"No."

"My pockets are full of notes I've written on napkins."

"This time *I'm* not surprised."

"I guess you wouldn't expect anything different." He'd let her believe whatever she wanted. It was just as well she wasn't impressed by him. Still, it would be nice...

Ty threw a couple of tens on the table. When Michelle started to argue he said, "Don't say anything about me paying. I'm the one who wanted to stop."

Outside, beside the motorcycle again, Michelle was determined to show Ty that she could handle the bike. She picked up her helmet before he had a chance to hand it to her. Pulling it into place and snapping the strap, she waited.

His grin gave her a surge of satisfaction. After he climbed on, she joined him, not hesitating to wrap her arms around him.

"I might have to start sabotaging your car every night if I get to have you hug me."

"I'm too tired to have a pithy comeback."

He chuckled. It made a wonderful ripple of sensation against her chest. Her nipples hardened in response. The man had a sexuality that called to her on a level she'd never experienced before. Her body hummed with an urge to answer. Maybe just this once. He wouldn't be here long. For once it could be about her. But she wouldn't. That road would lead to nothing but heartache. That alone made her determined not to need a ride from him again.

"Michelle, you're home. You can let go now." Ty shook his shoulder, jiggling her. His voice held a note of humor.

Oh, no. She had dozed off against Ty's back. She was so exhausted and he was so large, warm and comfortable she hadn't been able to keep her eyes from closing.

She jerked upright. "Uh, yeah."

"You were asleep, weren't you?"

She slid off the bike. Holding onto him as she went. She would miss not touching those powerful shoulders. "A little maybe. Thanks for the ride."

Ty put the kickstand down and began to climb off.

She removed her helmet and handed it to him.

"What're you doing?"

"Making sure you get inside safely."

"That's not necessary. I come in at all hours and have done so for years. I can take care of myself."

"Yes, ma'am. Just trying to be nice. Which one of these stately manors is yours?"

He made it sound like he wasn't impressed with the brick townhouses with the manicured shrubs. Once again she had the feeling he was scrutinizing her life and finding it lacking.

"The second on the right. Thanks again for the ride." She left him standing by the bike and headed for her front door. She pulled the key out of her scrub pants pocket, slipped it into the lock and was inside before she heard the roar of the motorcycle going down the road.

She couldn't remember the last time someone had waited outside her door to make sure she was in safely.

CHAPTER THREE

MICHELLE ROLLED OVER and picked up her phone. "Dr. Ross."

"Good afternoon, Michelle," Ty's deep-timbred voice said into her ear. Her treacherous heart leaped.

"Yes?"

"It's Ty."

"I know."

"Is that the best greeting you can give at two in the afternoon?"

"Yes."

He chuckled. "Not an afternoon person, are you?"

"Is there a problem with a patient?"

"No. I just wanted to let you know that I had Jimmy take care of your car."

"Jimmy?"

"Yeah, one of the hospital security guys. Fine fellow. He needs the extra money so I had him look at your car."

She'd worked at the hospital for years and she couldn't call a single security officer by name, but Ty knew all about one. Suddenly she felt ashamed of herself.

"Your car is running now. He says you shouldn't have any more problems. Just corroded cables."

"Uh, great. Thanks."

"You also left your purse in my bike. I've put it under the driver's seat of your car and locked it. Oh, by the way,

I had a look around and I now know your weight and how old you are."

"You did not!"

His full-bodied laugh covered her like a warm blanket from the dryer.

"I thought that might get a reaction. No, I didn't. But I did arrange for Jimmy to pick you up when you're ready. Just call Security and ask for him."

"I don't think—"

"Michelle, he needs the money. Let him have his pride."

Ty was really a good person. He saw a need and acted. She didn't say anything for a few seconds.

"Did you go back to sleep on me?"

A picture of her asleep with her head on his broad chest popped into her mind. "No," came out squeakier than she wished. "Thanks, Ty. I appreciate all you've done."

"No prob. See you soon."

Between her mother and her patients, she'd spent so much time taking care of others she forgotten just how nice it was to be taken care of. Too nice.

Four days later, Michelle was preparing to tap on the door of her patient's room when there was a burst of laughter from inside. Shawn had come through surgery well and after a short visit to CICU he was now in a room on the floor. She knocked.

A couple of deep voices could be heard then one called, "Come in."

She pushed the door open to find her patient sitting up in bed with a video-game controller in his hand. He didn't look at her. Instead, his focus remained on the bright animated characters on the TV. She glanced up to see what was happening. Every once in a while there was a white flash and a loud noise of something blowing up. Shaking her head, Michelle turned to her patient again.

Her eyes widened in disbelief. Sitting beside Shawn with another controller in his hand was Ty. She'd not seen him the last few days. With a sureness Michelle couldn't ignore, she admitted she'd missed him. Now he was shifting his body from side to side in an effort to see the TV around her.

"Dr. Ross, do you mind? I'm actually winning this time." Desperation and frustration filled his voice.

He was glad to see her too. Obviously not. She stepped to one side. Ty's actions weren't professional but from what she knew of him she would've wondered what was wrong with him if they had been.

"Thanks," Ty called to her. To Shawn he said, "You'd better move on or I'll overtake you." Ty moved his body one way and then the other as if he were the figure in the game.

Glancing at Shawn, she saw that he was making the same body movements. There was also a huge grin on his face. Michelle's heart lifted to see him enjoying himself. During the days before his surgery and those in CICU he'd been extremely depressed. He'd been so despondent that she'd worried it might affect his recovery. Ty had made the difference. For that she was grateful.

With a whoop of joy that Michelle thought might bring the nurses running the two men raised their hands over their heads.

"Once again you're the game master. Here I was helping Dr. Ross replace your heart valve and you repay me by beating the socks off me." Ty raised one hand higher and Shawn slapped it with his open palm.

Ty stood. The space in the room seemed to shrink. He was dressed in a pair of well-worn jeans and a T-shirt, with something ridiculous about "Ride a cycle and find a friend" written across his chest. He came to stand beside her.

"I'd better go and let Dr. Ross check you out. Maybe home will be on her agenda."

She smiled in agreement when Ty glanced over at her for confirmation. "It's very possible for tomorrow. Then you can get another game blaster."

Ty's laugh was deep and robust and was joined by Shawn's weaker one.

Warmth moved up her neck. Had she said something wrong?

"It's a game master." Ty said the last word carefully.

"Oh, I meant that."

Ty grinned and looked back at Shawn. "She's great with hearts but needs to get out more in the game department. You go home and rest up for our next match."

"I'll take you on any time, Ty."

Michelle liked to see that sign of feistiness. Shawn wanted to get well.

Ty smiled at Shawn. "I might not show it but I'm a poor loser. Next time you're mine, game *master*." Ty looked at her as if making a point then put out his fist. Shawn bumped it with his.

As he scooted passed her, Ty winked then went out the door. The special warmth that a man generated in a woman flared in her but just as quickly it turned into irritation. She wasn't some nurse, chasing him. She was the surgeon he worked with. How unprofessional! Suddenly all the positive thoughts she'd had about him went up in flames.

Of all the gall!

Fifteen minutes later she came out of Shawn's room pleased with her patient's progress. He would make a full recovery. Of course, he would always be a heart patient but Shawn had a chance to do and have anything a man his age wanted out of life. As she walked toward the nurses' station, she saw Ty talking to one of the staff. The woman looked at him as if he were a candy store and she loved sweets. Did every female find him fascinating?

She'd watched Ty work numerous times in surgery. He was respected professionally by both the males and females. His directives were followed without question but he could still interact on a personal level with the staff. They all seemed to like him. Was it just her that he rubbed the wrong way?

"Hey, Doc," he called as she started to pass. "Can I ask you something?"

Michelle tightened her lips for a second at the casual way he spoke to her. She was getting used to it but it still caught her off guard. No one else dared to speak to her the way he did. Her parents hadn't even called her by a nickname when she'd been growing up.

She approached him, glad the desk stood between them. He looked up at her from where he sat in a chair.

"Yes?"

"Tell me something, do you have any idea what a game master is?"

A sick, unsure feeling filled her. "Well, no."

"That's what I figured." He looked back down at the chart.

She waited but he didn't look up. His hair had fallen across his cheek so she couldn't tell if he might be looking at her. "Well?"

"Well, what?" His head rose and he considered her.

Ty picked then of all times to act serious. "Are you going to tell me what it is?" she snapped.

He grinned. "Oh, that. It's when you win at a video game. Shawn had to spend so much time taking it easy in the last few months that he's had plenty of time to get good at playing video games. He's a tough one to beat."

"I see." She didn't know if she should say the next words for fear he'd use them against her but she pressed on anyway. "You were really great with him the morning he went into surgery."

"I'm the last person he sees before he goes under. He might not have said it but he was afraid he wouldn't make it. He needed mine to be a friendly face."

She'd never thought about his job like that. "Still, I appreciate you taking so much time with him."

"Not a prob. He's a great kid who's had a lot of hard knocks."

Michelle wished she was that reassuring to her patients. She worked at not letting any emotion show. If it did, she was afraid it would overflow. She'd learned early on when her father had died the necessity of being strong. As a child it had been for her mother. In med school she'd had to be professional to survive. Now it was important that she always remain in control because her team followed her lead. Over the years it had become her demeanor, who she was. Who she had to be. She didn't know how to act any differently.

Could she be more unlike Ty if she tried?

"You're good at your job."

"Why, thank you, ma'am. I think am good at what I do too."

Why did he always manage to turn everything around so that it maddened her? "And you don't lack for an ego either," she said in a snippy tone.

"That wasn't ego talking."

"You're right. I can't fault your skill in the OR or with a patient. You have my sincerest apology for the way I acted on the day you arrived."

He presented her with a rakish grin. "Well, that was nice and unexpected. Would you mind insulting me again so I can hear you say 'I'm sorry' one more time?"

Ooh, the man made her want to slap that smile off his face while at the same time wanting to laugh. Instead, she turned and headed down the hall.

The sound of Ty's soft merriment followed her. He knew full well he'd gotten to her.

The day was beautiful. It was Ty's non-surgery one or what he typically called his "hate paperwork" day. He finished up with the two patients on the OR schedule for the next day and headed out to make the most of what was left of the hours before dark. Using a short cut he found by going through the women's center to where he parked his bike, he was looking forward to being outside.

Sunshine streamed through the two-story-high glass windows of the building. Waiting areas with low, modern seating in front of doctors' offices occurred every fifty feet or so. Green plants were placed artfully around the areas.

He'd almost reached the exit on the other end of the building when he saw Michelle. She was sitting next to a woman who had to be her mother, the resemblance was so strong.

He pulled up short and said, "Hi, Michelle."

She looked up from a magazine she'd been leafing through. Her eyes widened and she shifted in her chair. She wasn't pleased to see him. As he approached she glanced at the woman next to her. "Hello, Ty."

The older woman beside her watched their interchange with interest, looking between the two of them. He glanced at the woman.

"Uh, Ty, this is my mother, Betty Ross." Michelle acted as if she wasn't eager to introduce him.

He stepped forward and stretched out his hand. "It's a pleasure to meet you, Mrs. Ross. I'm Ty Smith."

Michelle's mother didn't stand but placed her fragile, pale hand in his. It was cool to the touch but there was warmth in her eyes. "Hello. Do you work with my daughter?"

"I do. She's an outstanding doctor."

He didn't miss the slight color that settled on Michelle's cheeks. Wasn't she used to being praised for her work? Or was it her looks that most people commented on?

"Why, thank you. I'm proud of her. She works so hard. Too hard, I think. So are you a doctor as well?"

As unsociable as Michelle acted, her mother went to the other extreme.

"Mom." Michelle's tone said she wished she could gracefully exit from the entire conversation. "I'm sure that Ty must have been on his way somewhere."

Ty ignored her blatant effort to get rid of him. He was enjoying talking to her mother and learning a little more about Michelle. She was so close-mouthed about anything related to her personal life that he'd been surprised to see her mother was still alive. "I'm an anesthesiologist. I work in the OR with your Michelle."

He didn't miss the tightening of Michelle's lips. Making her sound like a little girl didn't please her.

"Mrs. Ross," called a nurse from the door of an office.

Michelle's head jerked toward the voice before her gaze returned to meet his. There was a look of pain in her eyes but it disappeared when she blinked. That pain he didn't believe had anything to do with him. What was going on?

"Dr. Smith, it was nice to meet you. I hope we see each other again," Michelle's mother said softly.

"It would be a pleasure."

"Come on, Mom, the nurse is waiting."

Mrs. Ross rose slightly then sat down in the chair again as if she didn't have the strength to stand on her own.

"May I help you?" Ty asked, stepping forward and offering his arm.

"Thank you. I hate being so weak."

"Hold onto my arm and I'll support you as you stand up."

"I can do that." Michelle moved to the other side of her mother.

"I don't mind. In fact, I'd be honored." Ty didn't relinquish his place.

Mrs. Ross giggled like a young girl. "Michelle, I do believe your friend is a prince charming."

Ty winked at Michelle and grinned.

Michelle groaned, and his grin grew into a smile.

"Mrs. Ross, I take that as real praise coming from you." He helped her stand.

"How would you like to come to dinner some time?" Mrs. Ross asked him.

He glanced at Michelle. She looked appalled at the idea and as she opened her mouth to speak, Ty said, "I'd love to."

"Mother!" Michelle hissed.

Mrs. Ross ignored her and asked, "Tomorrow night?"

"That would be wonderful. I look forward to it." He looked past Mrs. Ross to find a resigned look on Michelle's face. "I'll get directions from Michelle."

"Mother, the nurse is waiting," she said in an exasperated voice laced with a tiredness that sounded bone deep.

Ty watched as Michelle assisted her mother into the office. He gaze rose to the large letters above the reception window. Oncology.

That was a tough diagnosis. No wonder Michelle could be difficult at times. She had to be worried about her mother.

Ty grinned at the look on Michelle's face as she opened the door of her mother's home the next evening. He'd had a warmer welcome from his cadaver in med school. "Good evening, Michelle."

"Come in," she murmured.

"Thank you for the heartfelt welcome."

"You know this wasn't my idea." She moved as if to make sure their bodies didn't touch as he entered.

"You've made that perfectly clear. But I'm glad your mother invited me. I'm going to enjoy having a home-cooked meal. It's something I don't often get."

She looked contrite. "I'm sorry. I'm not being very gracious. Come in. My mom is in the kitchen. I normally cook for her most evenings but she insisted on doing most of the meal tonight."

She closed the door behind them and he followed her to the kitchen. Michelle's mother's home was the kind that made him think of laughter and warm fires. It was as foreign to his growing-up years as he could imagine.

His life before Joey had really become sick had been carefree. He'd been encouraged to read and question but there had been little structure. Nothing permanent in his life other than his parents and Joey. In fact, he'd known nothing of his grandparents until he'd overheard his parents talking about them when he'd been around eight.

Ty paused to looked at the pictures in the hallway of Michelle at different stages in her life, some of them including her parents. There had been no family photos like these in his life. Heck, it was hard to hang a picture on the side of a tent.

When they entered the kitchen, Mrs. Ross turned away from the stove. She looked frail but there were red spots high on her cheeks. She wiped her hands and came towards him. "Welcome, Ty, I'm so glad you could join us."

"I appreciate being asked." He glanced at Michelle. She gave him more of a smirk than a smile.

"These are for you." He handed flowers and a long thin box to the older woman.

The red of her cheeks all but glowed with her pleasure as she took them. "Why, Ty, how sweet. You didn't have to."

"I wanted to."

"Michelle, honey, why don't you put these in a vase while I see what's in this pretty box? I can't imagine."

Michelle took the flowers and went to the sink.

Mrs. Ross opened the box and pulled out a multicolored scarf. "Oh, my, how beautiful." She wrapped it around her neck.

"I thought you might like it. My mother always said a bright scarf lifts a woman's spirits."

He'd not thought of that in a long time. Not quoted his parents in years. His mother had wrapped a red scarf around her head the day they'd marched out to bury Joey.

Ty's gaze shifted away from her mother to Michelle. Her eyes glistened and she mouthed, "Thank you," and gave him a smile. It was the first full-blown one he'd ever seen from her.

His eyes widened, he blinked and returned her smile with a wink.

"Michelle, why don't you take those flowers into the living room, and you and Ty have a little talk while I finish here? I won't be long."

Michelle looked as if she'd like to have the floor swallow her. He couldn't help but grin. This might be the most entertaining evening he'd spent in a long time.

She gathered the vase and without a backward glance headed back the way they had come. He followed, admiring the sensual sway of her hips. Did she have any idea what she could do to a man? This power was stronger than any she employed as a heart surgeon. She could rule the world. His, anyway.

When they got to the living room Michelle placed the flowers on the nearest table and turned to face him. "I'm sorry about this. I couldn't be more embarrassed."

"Hey, don't be. I'm flattered. I can't say that I know of another mother who has thrown her daughter at me."

He enjoyed the blush that covered her face. Yes, the ice queen had definitely melted.

Taking a seat on the sofa, he patted the cushion next to him. "Come sit and 'talk a little'."

Michelle sank next to him more out of defeat than anything else. He appreciated seeing her a little off center. The stiff doctor in control had all but been stripped away. She was just a daughter trying to make a sick mother happy.

"So your mother has cancer."

"Yes."

"How long?"

"We've been dealing with treatments for the last six months."

"That has to have been tough. On both of you."

"It has been. I have all this medical knowledge but I can't help her. What good is it all if you can't save the people you love?"

A stab of pain filled him. What would have happened if he'd defied his parents and taken Joey for help? He knew too well what it meant to watch a loved one die. He carried the guilt daily.

"So what is the prognosis?"

"Mom seems to be doing well medically but I worry over her depression. Tonight is the first time in months that she's been this animated and energetic."

"So the way to perk her up is to see you interested in a guy?"

Michelle shifted away. "I'm not interested in you."

Ty took her hand in his and rubbed his thumb across the

top of it. He turned it over to where he could feel the whip of her pulse under the delicate skin covering her wrist. "Are you sure about that?"

She pulled her hand away. "I appreciate you making my mother happy but I don't plan to play the game any further than tonight."

Was he playing a game? No, he didn't think so. Suddenly he wanted to get to know this beautiful, complicated woman better. Careful, that idea sounded too much like getting involved. That, he wouldn't let happen. They could be friends. Have a few laughs while he was in town but that was it.

"Ever thought that I might find you interesting? Want to get to know you better?"

"No. Why would you? I'm not your type. We are too different. We barely tolerate each other."

"I think we're tolerating each other just fine now."

And they were. In fact, it had been a long time since he'd just enjoyed talking to a woman without there being any expectation on the part of either side.

Mrs. Ross stuck her head into the room. "Dinner is served."

Michelle shot to her feet as if her mother had seen them doing something she didn't want her to know about. He stood more slowly.

Michelle's heart caught and fluttered back into rhythm. Maybe there was more to Ty than she'd given him credit for. At least her mother was happier than she'd seen her in a long time. For that alone Michelle could tolerate him for an evening.

She followed her mother back into the kitchen. Michelle came to an abrupt stop, causing Ty to bump into her. His hand touched her waist briefly, steadying her.

Her mother had set her father's place for Ty.

"You okay?" he asked next to her ear. If her mother turned round now she'd think there truly was something between them. They stood so intimately close.

"Yeah."

"Ty, this is your place." Her mother indicated her father's chair.

"Thank you, ma'am," Ty said as he sat. "This looks wonderful and smells even better." Michelle sank into her chair. She watched as Ty's well-manicured hands picked up his napkin and shook it out then placed it in his lap.

His hand touching hers under the table jerked her attention to his eyes. She smiled and shook off the melancholy. He removed his hand. It was past time to let her father's place go. Maybe even other things about him. Her mother certainly needed to move on after so many years. Had they both been caught up in a void that they needed to get beyond?

"Michelle, why don't you serve Ty some roast?"

Ty picked up his plate and offered it to her. His eyes still held a concerned look. He saw things about her that others never noticed. Far too often.

She dished up the meat and her mother passed him the bowl of mashed potatoes. The two of them carried on a conversation as if they were old friends, leaving Michelle time to observe Ty.

He might be the most handsome man she'd ever seen. At first she'd thought his hair was too much but the better she got to know him the more she thought it suited him. Combed back, the ends curled around the back of his neck. Tonight he was wearing a collared shirt of tiny green plaid that made his eyes seem darker. His pants were well-pressed tan cotton twill. She couldn't fault his appearance in any way.

Even in the OR she'd started to look forward to seeing what kind of outrageous scrub cap he might wear next. She'd also noticed his original lime-colored clogs were exchangeable for bright orange ones on occasion.

"Michelle…" Her mother's note of irritation implied she must have called her name more than once.

"Why don't you clear the dishes and bring that apple pie over here? There's also ice cream in the freezer."

"Okay, how many nights of the week can I eat here?" Ty asked.

Michelle almost dropped the dishes.

Thankfully her mother just giggled, instead of telling him Monday, Wednesday and Friday.

Michelle placed the pie in the middle of the table and returned for the ice cream as Ty said, "You're a great cook, Mrs. Ross. That was some of the best food I've ever eaten."

"I love to cook. I even thought about opening a tearoom when Michelle was a small child but there never seemed to be time."

That was news to Michelle. A tearoom. Her mother hadn't cooked for herself in weeks. Michelle had thought she'd forgotten how until tonight.

"I'm sure you would've made a success of it."

"I'm too old to do that now but I do still love to go to tea."

Michelle had forgotten about that as well. Before she'd become sick her mother had gone out with her friends regularly. These days she didn't go out except when she had a doctor's appointment.

Soon after dessert Ty said he must be going. Michelle wondered if he had someplace else to be or someone else he was meeting. He didn't strike her as a home body who spent a lot of time by himself. Why she cared she didn't know, but she did.

"Michelle, why don't you see Ty to the door?"

She made an effort not to roll her eyes.

Ty graciously thanked her mother and followed Michelle out of the kitchen. She opened the front door and Ty brushed her arm as he moved his large body past hers. A tingle of heat went through her as if she had been branded. She had to stop overreacting to his slightest touch.

She stepped out onto the porch and closed the door behind them. "I'm sorry about tonight. I had no idea that she was going to put you on the spot."

"Hey, don't worry about it. I enjoyed being here. There's nothing wrong with a parent caring about their child and showing it. Your mother just wants you to be happy."

"I know, but tonight's show said that we'd stepped back thirty years or more in dating time."

"Didn't liked me being pushed at you, did you?" He chuckled.

"I was mortified."

"It was a compliment."

He really was understanding about a number of things now that she'd thought about it. "Well, I appreciate you being okay with it. My mom seemed to enjoy having you to dinner and that's something she hasn't done in a long time."

"And how about you? Did you enjoy having me?"

He made the question sound so suggestive that she felt as if her temperature had spiked. "I'm not sure what you mean."

Ty's eyes studied her for far longer than was comfortable before he said in a low, rusty voice, "I think you probably do but don't want to admit it."

It was exciting to have Ty's complete attention. He made her feel things long locked away, even those she'd never felt before. Would it really be so bad to have a fling with him? After all, he would be gone in a few weeks.

His attention was captured by something behind her. "Your mother is looking out the window. Let's not disappoint her."

His arm circled her waist, bringing her against him. Michelle didn't even try to struggle, her hands going to rest lightly on his shoulders. With her height, Ty was only a few inches taller than she was. He had a slight grin on his mouth as he looked into her eyes and brought his lips down to touch hers. Ty smelled of apples, cinnamon and coffee. Her breath slowed as his full and mobile mouth pressed firmly against hers.

Heat flowed through her blue-flame hot. When had been the last time she'd been kissed? Had any kisses ever made her feel the way this one did?

Her fingers dug into his shoulders. Ty's tightened his arm, bringing her closer. His other hand rose to circle the back of her neck. He guided her head so that he captured her mouth more fully.

Just as Michelle began to press closer he pulled away. Disappointment swamped her. She wanted more. Stumbling slightly, Ty steadied her.

"That should make your mother happy."

What? Michelle sucked in her breath. She'd experienced the kiss of her life and Ty had only done so to make her mother happy! Could she be more insulted?

She jerked out of his arms. "If I didn't care that my mother was watching, I'd slap your face."

With that, she re-entered the house, leaving Ty standing on the porch.

CHAPTER FOUR

TY'S GAZE LIFTED away from the blood-pressure monitor to Michelle. She was engrossed in watching the resident remove the cannula running to the heart-lung machine as they took their patient, a sixty-three-year-old female, off bypass in the OR.

He didn't understand her reaction two nights before when he'd kissed her. He'd made a mistake somewhere. Not usually so out of tune with a woman, Michelle's response to his kiss had thrown him. He'd thought she'd been enjoying it. He certainly had been. With her mother watching, he hadn't been able to take it as far as he wished.

The ice queen had returned, North-Pole cold this morning. She wouldn't even look at him and if she did it was to ask a question necessary to patient care only. Normally he'd have shrugged her displeasure off and moved on but Michelle had gotten to him on a level he'd never known before. He didn't like things not being right between them.

The resident tipped the heart up to get a look at the suture line on the back.

"BP dropping. Eighty over sixty. That's enough," Ty called.

The resident put the heart back in place.

"BP coming up. You guys know that makes me nervous when you do that."

Michelle and the resident weren't really listening to him. They had their heads together, looking intently into the chest of the patient.

"Where is that blood coming from?" she asked no one in particular. "What is the ACT?" she demanded, without looking at him.

"Normal range," Ty answered, letting her know that the activated clotting time was fine. Before he'd started the patient on bypass, using the heart-lung machine, he'd given her blood thinner. When the patient had come off bypass he'd had to reverse it by giving protamine.

"Do more factors need to be given?"

"No. Platelets and FFP are in range," Ty responded. He checked again. Nothing indicated fresh frozen plasma was needed.

"What does the TEG show?"

The TEG was a research tool that told him what part of the clotting cascade was deficient. "Numbers are good."

"Then we are prolene-deficient," Michelle announced.

Ty jerked his head up to look at her. More sutures were required. Her voice was higher than normal. She was rattled for some reason.

"Let's find this thing," she snapped. "We need to know if it's the suture line or a vessel.

"Pack it with sponges and see what we get."

The resident began to place sponges around the heart. Then they waited.

For the first time her eyes met Ty's. Her gaze remained long enough for him to see the terror in her eyes.

"BP?" she asked.

"Dropping slowly."

"Let's get them out," she said, referring to the sponges.

The resident removed one from behind the heart. It was bright red. "Got it."

"The arterial suture line," Michelle said, with less confidence than she usually showed . "I thought I'd put in enough stitches."

He couldn't see her eyes but her breathing had become more rapid. Ty checked the monitors to make sure all was well on his end before he looked up. This was supposed to be a straightforward bypass case, something that Michelle could do in her sleep.

Done with adding stitches, she stood, her eyes transfixed on the chest of the patient. She didn't move. Didn't say anything.

"Michelle," Ty said in a firm tone.

She blinked then turned to the resident. "Can you close?"

He nodded.

Ty could see moisture filling her eyes. Why had this case gotten to her so? He didn't miss the shock on the faces of the other team members.

Jane, her scrub nurse, asked, "Dr. Ross, are you okay?"

Michelle didn't answer as she exited the OR.

"Call the scrub desk and have Dr. Marcus come in and finish up for me," he told his nurse.

Ty was only minutes behind Michelle. He found her in the locker room, sitting on a bench. She had removed her mask and tears showed on her cheeks. Michelle looked around as if she didn't know which way to go. She wouldn't like the staff seeing her going into meltdown. He jerked his mask off and grabbed her wrist. "Come with me."

He led her out of the OR suite to the employee elevator and pushed the up button. Thankfully they didn't have to wait long for the elevator doors to open.

"Where're we going?" Good. She was coming back from that dark place.

"I'll show you."

"Ty, this isn't the time for one of your games. I just want to be left alone."

"This isn't one of my games." He was glad to see they had reached the top floor. When the doors opened he took her hand. She didn't make any attempt to refuse it. That alone told him how upset she was.

When she started to speak he said, "Hush and follow me." He circled around the elevator and pushed open the door to the roof.

"What're we doing here?"

"I always find a place to go just so I can breathe. This is my place and I think you could use it today."

"How do you get past Security?" The pragmatic Michelle had returned. That was an encouraging sign. For a second there he'd been concerned for her emotional health.

"I made a deal with Jimmy."

"Figures. Why're you doing this? You're not my new best friend," she said, pulling her hand out of his. This feistiness was better than what he'd seen in her eyes earlier.

"What happened in there?"

"Nothing. We had a bleeder. We found it. All in a day of surgery."

That statement was too flippant, coming from Michelle. "I know better. Spill. Is it your mother?"

"Why would you think that?"

"Sixty-three-year-old female. Could have died. That's who our patient is. Sound like any one you know? I don't have to be a mind-reader to get the connection."

"All brilliant deductions, Doctor. Yes. This one hit a bit too close to home," she said with disgust.

Whether or not it was the situation or her, he didn't know. He moved to where he could look out over the city, pleased she followed. If he could get her to talk, maybe he could help. He may be taking an interest in Michelle's problems, but he wouldn't be there for her for the long haul. She didn't need to come to depend on him.

When she came to stand beside him he said, "Makes you feel like the king of the mountain to be up here. As if you have some control over someone's life if not your own."

She glanced at him. "What do you know about not having control? You go through life as if it is a fun ride at a carnival."

"Take my word for it. I know it isn't. Talk to me, Michelle."

"I don't want to talk about it." She kicked at the gravel covering the top on the roof with the toe of her shoe. It reminded him of a little girl on the playground unsure if she should climb the monkey bars.

"But I think you need to. What gives?"

"What gives? Are you a hippy?"

"No, but I was raised by some hippy wannabes. But that isn't what we are here to discuss."

"What do you want to hear? I fell apart in the OR because the patient reminded me of my mother. Happy now?"

"Okay, but why?"

"Stop pushing, Ty."

"Why? Your mother is getting better."

She rounded on him. "Because I'm afraid she might die. I've already lost a father. I don't have anyone else."

She had isolated herself so completely that she had no one to turn to. "Your team has no idea your mother has been sick, do they?"

Michelle lowered her eyes and shook her head.

"You need to talk to them. When the surgeon breaks down over a patient, it unnerves the team. I knew it was serious when they all looked at you like a deer in the headlights. Not one of them blinked. They're not used to that type of emotion from you. And they had no idea where it came from."

"I didn't get the name ice queen for nothing," she retorted.

"I'm sorry. I know that must hurt."

She shrugged.

He took her by the shoulders. "You need to tell them what's going on in your life. They're your friends. They'll want to help. I want to help. Let me."

"You can't. It's not something that you can laugh off and make okay."

His hands dropped away from her. "That's a little harsh, even for you, Michelle."

She had the good grace to look contrite. "I'm sorry. That was uncalled for."

"You're upset. Why have you kept your mother's issue hidden?"

"Because I'm the surgeon, the leader. I have to be strong."

"Agreed, but you are also human. Your mother is sick. You have every right to be upset. Patients and the people you work with also need to know you are human too."

"Are you saying I'm not?"

"No, if anything I think you're too human. Feel too much. You just refuse to show it. Are *afraid* to show it."

She turned her back to him. Her shoulders slumped.

Ty wrapped his arms around her and pulled her against him. Her head rolled back to rest on his chest. "Aw, sweetheart, this too will pass. Cry it out and you'll feel better."

He might not. The more he knew about Michelle the more difficult it was going to be to leave in a few weeks. But leave he would. He always did.

Michelle sat reviewing a chart of one of her patients at the nurses' station on the floor. Her mind wasn't on what she was doing, as it should've been. Instead, it was on the last conversation she'd had with Ty. She didn't know if she would ever be able to face him again. He'd seen through her!

She'd come unglued and he'd been there to witness it. After she'd recovered from her crying jag, they'd returned to the OR suite. She'd immediately spoken to the resident about the patient. He'd informed her that woman was doing well and was comfortable in CICU.

At least today she didn't have any surgeries so she wouldn't have to face Ty just yet.

"Did you hear about Ty?" one of the nurses told another in a raised voice. "He was hit in the parking lot this morning on his way in. He's in Emergency,"

Michelle's heart dropped to her stomach. She put her hands in her lap to stop the shaking. The sudden urge to run to the ER filled her.

"Is he badly hurt?" one of the nurses asked, so Michelle didn't have to.

"I don't know. I just saw all the commotion and a motorcycle on the ground. A couple of ER staff were there. That's all I know."

Michelle bit her lip and forced herself not to make a scene by jumping up and rushing to the ER. Logging out of the computer, she tried to act as normally as possible while her heart raced. All that went through her head was wondering how badly he'd been hurt.

The emergency room wasn't a place that Michelle frequented. In fact, she had to follow the signs to find her way through the maze of hallways. When she arrived at the ER she was grateful for the lab coat that instantly identified her as a doctor and therefore gained her attention from the staff. The nurse at the desk looked up at Michelle, who asked, "Which room is Ty Smith in?"

The nurse looked at her as if she wasn't sure about Michelle's tone but checked the large chart on the wall. "Room four." She pointed down the hall.

At the door Michelle hesitated. What was she doing? What if Ty didn't want her there? She convinced herself he'd only been being kind to her mother and her and that he had no one else in town… Who was she kidding? She was worried about him.

Tapping lightly, she pushed the door open.

"Oh, my God, Ty. Are you okay?" She hurried to the stretcher.

"Hey, Michelle." He gave her a weak smile. That worried her more than anything. She'd never seen him with less than a cheerful grin.

"Don't look so scared. It looks far worse than it is."

She couldn't imagine that being true. His right arm was covered in gauze from wrist to elbow. On the other side there was a bandaged area on his upper arm and one covering his palm. His scrub pants had been cut away and there was a bandage around his knee, along with other scrapes and bruises. It looked as if his helmet had done its job. His gorgeous face didn't have a scratch on it.

"I told you motorcycles were dangerous." She touched his hand. He curled a bloody finger around one of hers then grimaced with the movement.

"I do think you mentioned that."

"Are there any bones broken?"

"Nope. A few stitches. Bruises and a possible concussion. I'm going to be out of commission for a few days, so I guess you won't have to worry about me being late."

"Not funny, Ty."

"Why, Michelle, if I didn't know better, I'd think you might care."

"Come on, Ty. You're hurt. I'd have to be heartless not to."

"It might be worth losing my bike just to get this kind of attention from you." He chuckled then winced.

There was a sharp knock at the door and a woman in scrubs with a lab coat covering them entered the room. She put out her hand and Michelle shook it. "I heard you were here, Dr. Ross. I'm Dr. Lassiter. We don't see heart surgeons down here much." She turned her attention to Ty. "In fact, this is more of the OR staff than we've seen in years. Busy morning for us. Dr. Smith, you'll be away from work for a couple of days. You'll also need help at home. Do you have anyone who can see about you?"

"I'll take care of him," Michelle said with conviction.

Ty's brows rose.

Even she was surprised by her lack of thought where that offer was concerned.

"Great. Then I'll get the paperwork started so you can take him home," Dr. Lassiter said in a pleased voice, and left.

Home! Ty would be staying at her house. Their last meeting had ended with her squalling all over him and now she was going to have him living with her. If she hadn't already been having trouble with her emotions where he was concerned, she certainly would now.

But he needed her help and she couldn't refuse. When she'd opened her mouth to say she'd care for him she'd jumped in at the deep end.

"Having second thoughts, are you?"

She met Ty's look.

"I can see it written all over your face."

He was starting to make her angry. Always thinking he could read her mind. She'd managed her feelings and had been getting along just fine until this handsome hunk of a man had come roaring into town.

She straightened her back and gave him a direct look. "No, I was just thinking about what I needed to do to make you comfortable. I don't have guests often."

"I'd bet you haven't had a sleepover in a long time."

"You make this sound like a slumber party."

His eyes grew darker. "Slumbering with you has its appeal."

"Yeah, you look like you went five rounds with a car and you're out. I don't think you'll be chasing me around the condo. If I had to guess, sleeping is all you'll be doing for a day or so."

"That cut to the quick." He sequenced his face as if he were hurt.

"You do have some luck. It's Friday evening and we're both off this weekend."

His eyes turned serious. "I'd hate you to spend your days off seeing to me."

"Who else is going to?"

"I'll be all right by myself."

The ER doctor entered just in time to hear his remark.

"If you don't have someone with you then I'll admit you. You have a possible concussion. Someone has to be with you for at least the first twenty-four hours."

"Whoa, I don't do hospitals," Ty said.

"What? You work in a hospital." Michelle couldn't believe the distress she heard in his voice.

"But I'm not a patient."

Michelle looked at Dr. Lassiter and they both said at the same time, "Men."

"Don't worry. He's going home with me," Michelle told the other woman.

"Good. Here's his release form and instructions. You'll

need to stay with him. The pain med is going to make him sleepy but you need to wake him up every couple of hours. Make him talk to you."

"Hello. I'm right here," Ty said, as if he were a little boy trying to get his mother's attention so he could lick the cake beaters.

"You're not going to remember any of this so Dr. Ross needs to know," the ER doctor told him calmly. To Michelle she said, "I think you'll have your hands full."

Michelle was afraid of that.

Less than an hour later Michelle watched closely as Ty climbed the three steps as she opened the door to her condo.

"Wow, I never expected all this color. Like your office. This is the hidden Michelle." He looked at her. "I like it."

Michelle was sure she turned pink. His reaction pleased her. "You can admire or analyze my home later. Right now I need to get you to bed."

"Great. You say that when I'm so sore and drugged up I can't act on it."

"Come on, funny guy. I'll show you where you can stay."

She directed him down the hall to the spare room, which she'd decorated in lively colors and *avant-garde* paintings. "The bath is through there." She pointed to a smaller door to the right. "I'll let you get settled then be back to check on you. Holler if you need anything." She gathered the decorative pillows off the bed and placed them in a chair, before pulling the covers back.

Ty looked at her. "Really, Michelle, thanks for doing this. Hopefully I'll be out of your hair by tomorrow."

"Someone has to take care of you."

He chuckled. "That's my Michelle, the woman with the warm heart."

"I'm not your woman."

He headed toward the bathroom. "Maybe not yet."

Ty woke with a start. He shifted in bed and groaned. Every muscle ached and it seemed that every inch of his skin hurt. He looked around, trying to remember where he was. The room was dim but he could make out the teal shade of the wall and the splashes of color of the pictures on it. Michelle's.

He vaguely remembered crawling between cool sheets and closing his eyes. He pushed the cover back and winced. He would have liked to have been invited over to Michelle's but he wouldn't have gone to this extreme to gain an invitation. The slide across the pavement had done a number on him. At least he'd been wearing his helmet or it would have been worse. He kicked to get unbound from the bed sheets. Despite the pain medicine he'd taken, he'd still tossed and turned. He'd appreciate some painkillers right now.

He focused on a painting of a beach scene in yellow, blue and red. Michelle's place had not just surprised him, it had been a shock. As conservative as she appeared on the outside, her home, along with her office, was filled with color. Here the furniture leaned toward ultra-modern, chrome and glass tables mixed with wooden chairs painted blue. Who would have thought Michelle was a closet color fiend? Her traditional conservative suits in pale colors hid a woman with flair.

Rolling his head to the side, his eyes widened when he saw Michelle sitting in a cushioned chair next to the bed. She was asleep.

Her hair was loose and a lock fell across one eye. She wore knit pants and a sweatshirt with striped socks on her feet. Her clothes in no way detracted from her beauty.

He'd not thought about her good looks in a number of days. Trying to keep up with her sharp wit had occupied his mind. Her house just added one more personality trait for him to contemplate. The woman was an interesting combination of contradictions. He never knew what he would get next.

Moving his neck to work out some of the soreness, he looked around further and found the bedside clock. It was four in the morning.

"Michelle," he said hoarsely. The pain medicine had made his mouth dry. He cleared his throat and called her name again with more strength.

Her eyes opened with alarm and she jerked upwards.

"You need to go bed or you're going to be in worse shape than me from sitting in that chair."

Michelle looked at the clock. "It's time for your medicine. I'll get it."

She didn't wait for him to object before she stood and headed out of the room.

He watched her stride away. She had such an amazingly sexy walk. His eyelids drifted downwards.

A gentle but warm hand resting on his shoulder shook him.

Michelle's face was close enough that she had to have been studying his face before she'd woken him. Ty's blood heated and flowed to a part of him that had nothing to do with the accident and everything to do with being so close to Michelle.

Her hand move to touch his forehead.

"Ty, you need to sit up and take your medicine. You're running a low-grade fever."

"My head hurts."

"I'm not surprised. I bet you hit it hard when you fell."

He put his hands out on either side of his hips to push himself into a sitting position. He let out a grunt and Michelle rushed to put an arm around his waist.

He sure wished he felt well enough to really appreciate her touch.

"Let me help."

Between the two of them they managed to get him into enough of a sitting position that he could swallow the meds with the water without it running down his face.

When Michelle didn't say anything or move away, he looked at her. Her gaze was focused on his lap. The covers had slipped down during their efforts to get him into the correct position. And had dropped indecently low. His privates remained covered but it was clear he was nude.

"You don't have any clothes on." The words were a small squeak for Michelle.

"Don't wear them to bed."

Michelle's creamy skin had turned a charming pink and her gaze remained at his waist. Under such scrutiny and obvious fascination, his manhood began to show its appreciation. He reached down and pulled the covers up above his waist.

She deserved better than a lover who couldn't give his best because his body wasn't in a good state. He groaned as he moved. What he wouldn't give for a cold bath! Maybe that would ease the roar of desire in him. He wanted Michelle with a fierceness he'd rarely known.

"In a hundred years I couldn't explain how much I hate feeling so rough right now because that type of admiration should be rewarded. Instead, I think you should make a straight line to your bedroom and lock the door."

Michelle gulped and her eyes flew to meet his gaze. Her hand shook as she offered him the rest of the glass of water. He drank it all. Some dribbled down his chin and she wiped it away.

Ty reached up and grabbed her wrist. Taking the cloth

napkin out of her hand, he opened her fingers and kissed the center of her palm. "Thanks for taking care of me."

Michelle drew in a breath then let it out slowly. She nodded, picked up his medicine and left. As his eyelids drifted closed he again enjoyed the sight of the sway of her hips.

"Wake up."

Ty's eyelids flickered upwards. His eyes strained in an effort to focus on Michelle. Once again she was sitting in the chair beside his bed.

"What's your name?"

"You know my name."

"Tell me your name. I need to know you don't have a concussion."

"Ty Smith. And you are Michelle Ross. And you're not holding up any fingers."

"Funny, very funny."

"I told you to go to bed."

Her eyes didn't leave his. "Can't. I have to see about you."

"Well, I'm not going back to sleep until you lie down."

"I need to be close so I can check on you. I'm fine in this chair."

He shifted closer to the edge of the bed and patted the other side. "If you're not going to your bed then you have to share mine."

"I'm not sharing the bed with you!"

"Hey, it hurts like the devil to move. I'm not going to do anything. I'm not even capable of sitting up without a struggle. Who are you more afraid of, me or you?" He grinned at her huff of indignation. "That's what I thought. Lie down on top of the spread and pull that quilt at the end of the bed up over you. That way we both can get some sleep." He gave her his best determined look.

She stood. "Okay, if you promise to go back to sleep."

"Frankly, I'd love to kiss you all over but, much as I hate to admit it, I don't think I'd be at my best," he murmured in a gravelly voice. "So as soon as you're settled I'll go straight to sleep."

Michelle walked around the bed. She stood looking down at the space he'd offered for so long he thought she wasn't going to do as he asked. Finally, she sat down, pulled the quilt up and lay down.

"Hey, don't move around too much. It rocks the bed. Hurts," he mumbled as he closed his eyes.

She went so still she gave a new meaning to the saying "as stiff as a board" but at least she'd get some decent sleep. He liked knowing she was near far too much.

CHAPTER FIVE

MICHELLE CARESSED THE smooth, heated silk beneath her hand. Mmm. It felt wonderful. She liked fine sheets and pillow cases but this one was extra special. She rubbed her cheek against it. Perfect.

Her eyes opened, to be captured by green ones that didn't blink. The pain that had fogged Ty's eyes the night before had disappeared, to be replaced by desire that was crystal clear.

She tingled with want. Her fingers flexed against the skin of Ty's waist and her cheek rested on his upper arm. Michelle wanted to groan but clapped her mouth closed. Hadn't she already embarrassed herself enough?

With a jerk, she sat up. Glancing at Ty, she found his gaze still on her. Why didn't he say something? Defuse the tension, as thick as ice, between them? He'd always made jokes. Where was one when she needed it?

"I'll, uh, get your medicine."

"Michelle?"

She stood and pushed her clothes back into place.

"Yes?"

"I couldn't think of a nicer way to wake up."

She shoved her hair back, hoping it was going into some semblance of order. "I bet you say that to all the women."

His look intensified, bored into hers. "I do not."

Heat flared in her. It felt good to be considered special by this man. "I'll get you something to eat."

"I'd rather have you," he said softly as she went through the door.

Michelle headed straight to her room and into the bathroom. She looked in the mirror. Her face was flushed as if she were a teenage girl who'd received her first kiss. And Ty hadn't even tried!

She'd been the one caressing his chest. The one who had rolled towards him. How could her body have betrayed her like that?

But it had been an extremely pleasant feeling to have Ty look at her with desire. What if she took him up on his interest? Would it be so bad to let go for a while? They were both adults…

All those romantic thoughts amounted to nothing. He was only interested because she'd all but thrown herself at him in her sleep. He'd made it clear the other night that he'd only kissed her for the benefit of her mother.

Enough of that. Ty had been injured and still needed care. Starting with something to eat. Heck, she'd been so caught up in her attraction to him she'd not even asked him how he was feeling. He managed to get her to forget everything but how he made her feel.

She washed her face and pulled a brush through her hair.

In the kitchen, she started the coffeemaker and pulled out eggs, bacon, cheese and bread. She was in the process of putting together an omelet when Ty entered the room.

All he wore was the bottoms to a scrub set. He'd been given a new pair in the ER to come home in as a leg had been cut out of his other ones. In fact, that's all he had to wear. Her hand shook as she picked up the whisk to whip the eggs. She beat them far too vigorously in an effort not to stare.

Had Little Red Riding Hood felt this unsure when she'd faced the wolf? That was a foolish thought. She was a grown woman and a doctor who saw people undressed regularly. For heaven's sake, she was acting like a silly schoolgirl seeing her first naked chest. The problem was that it wasn't bare chests that got to her, it was Ty's in particular and it being in her kitchen. Few she'd seen before were as muscular or well defined as Ty's.

"How're you feeling?" she croaked.

He gingerly put a hip on a bar stool. "I'm stiff. I needed to move around a bit."

"Well, don't start thinking you're well enough to do as you please."

"I promise to be a model patient," he said with a weak smile.

"You can start being that by taking your meds and eating all your breakfast. I'll have it ready in a minute."

She put her back to him. Placing a pan on the eye of the stove, she turned it on to heat. She didn't have to look at Ty to know that he was watching her. Every fiber in her body was aware of his appraisal. The hair on her arms stood on end.

Minutes later, she placed a plate with a cheese omelet, bacon and toast in front of Ty.

He inhaled deeply. "This smells and looks wonderful." He cut into the eggs and forked them into his mouth. "Just wish it took less effort to eat."

"Would you like me to feed you?" Michelle asked.

He twisted his lip up in disgust. "I'm in bad enough shape without having the humiliation of being fed like a baby. Hey, you do know that a way to a man's heart is through his stomach?"

What would it be like to have Ty's heart? To wake up every morning touching him? Being touched?

She returned to cooking her food in the hope that Ty might think the heat in her cheeks was coming from the stove. "I've heard that but I'm only interested in getting you well enough that you can make you own breakfast," she said over her shoulder.

"Hey, I don't take up that much room."

Yes, he did. He filled every room he was in as far as she was concerned.

They ate in silence until Michelle said, "I'll need to take a look at those stitches as you ran a fever last night."

"I figured as much. I hate to ask it but I think the bandage on my knee needs some attention as well. It has bled through."

"As soon as we're done here I'll see about getting you cleaned up and then you can get back into bed. You look as if you're fading fast."

"I'll have to admit I'm not feeling as energetic as I'd like to be. Thanks for the food. I'm going to wash before you see about my bandages."

She put her plate in the sink then picked up Ty's and did the same. "I'll straighten up and be there in a few minutes."

Killing as much time as she could to make sure Ty was out of the bathroom, she knocked lightly on the door to his bedroom fifteen minutes later.

"Michelle, could you help me?" Ty called from the direction of the bathroom.

She didn't think twice before she hurried towards his voice. "Are you all right? What have you done?"

Ty stood near the tub with the shower curtain pulled back. A towel was wrapped around his waist.

"What're you doing? You can't get in the tub with those bandages on."

"I wasn't going to get in the tub. I sponged off the best I could and I was just going to wet my hair so I could wash it. But I decided that wasn't such a good idea. Could you help me?"

Michelle smiled. He sounded pitiful. "Why didn't you ask me sooner?"

"I don't know. Somehow it doesn't sound too macho to ask a woman to wash your hair."

She laughed genuinely this time. "Turn the water off."

He did as he was told then looked at her questioningly.

"Put your pants back on. Customers don't get a wash and dry in my beauty shop dressed in a towel. Meet me in the kitchen."

Ty dropped the towel to the floor and struggled into his scrub pants again. Barefoot, he padded to the kitchen. It hurt just to walk but he knew he'd feel better if he was at least clean. Michelle stood by the sink with towels and a bottle of shampoo at hand.

"So did you work your way through school in a beauty shop?" he asked.

"No, but my mother used to wash my hair like this all the time. You have enough that it needs to be done this way."

"Are you complaining about the length of my hair?" he asked in as indignant a tone as he could muster.

"No. I've never seen more beautiful hair."

Her sharp intake of breath told him she hadn't meant to say that. He grinned. Thankfully that didn't cause any pain. "Why, thank you, ma'am. I always hated it. Too curly, like a girl's."

"I know more than one girl who wished she had hair like yours." Michelle suddenly turned businesslike and folded up a towel lengthways and placed it on the counter in front of the sink. She turned on the faucet.

"Now you're starting to embarrass me. Let's get on with

this." He glanced at her. Had she said she didn't think that was possible?

After testing the water with her hand, Michelle said, "Lean over the sink. Put your chest against the counter." She pulled out the hand sprayer. "You might want to close your eyes."

He leaned forward from the waist and felt every muscle in his body. He moaned.

"I'm sorry. You must be very sore. I'll make this as quick as I can."

Warm water hit his head and Michelle's fingers ran along his scalp, fanning out and moving through his hair.

"Turn your head the other way," Michelle said in a soft voice that sounded as wonderful as the spray felt.

When the water stopped he groaned.

"Are you in pain?"

"No. Not if I don't move. I moaned because that felt so good."

She laughed quietly. "I used to complain too when Mother turned off the water."

He started to stand.

She placed a hand between his shoulder blades. "Stay where you are."

The heat of it was like a brand on his skin. Her fingertips trailed away.

He looked at the sink drain and waited. The top of what had to be the shampoo popped then there was a squirting sound.

"Here." She handed him a small towel. "I don't want to get any soap in your eyes so hold it over your face."

Seconds later her fingers begin tunneling through his hair. Slowly her fingertips massaged their way across his scalp. She applied pressure and he sighed with pleasure as she worked her way up and over the crown of his head.

Coming back down, she took extra time at the base of his neck in an almost erotic movement of her fingers.

"Mmm, that feels good."

She giggled lightly and scrubbed with more force, using the ends of her fingers.

Ty closed his eyes and enjoyed the sensation, forgetting about any pain. The pressure ended. "Hey, don't stop now. That feels so great."

She chuckled. He moved as if to stand and she said, "Be still or you'll get soap everywhere."

A second later spray, warmer than before, hit the top of his head and flowed downwards.

Michelle's fingers returned to moving gently through his hair as she removed the suds. Far too soon, she turned off the water. "Stay still. I'm not done yet."

A towel flapped over his head and she began to gently rub his hair dry. She was as thorough and precise at hair washing as she was in the OR.

He shifted and looked her direction. One of her breasts was within an inch of his lips. His mouth went dry.

"Stop moving."

Had she caught him?

"Turn your head."

Disappointment filled him at losing such a delightful view. Adulation replaced his regret when both breasts were pressed firmly against his shoulder as she leaned over to get to the top of his head. Grateful to be on the receiving end of all this attention, Ty hated to see it end. He'd had no idea how pleasurable it was to have someone wash his hair. Especially if it was Michelle.

"You can straighten up now."

Ty did so but far too stiffly. Did he look as pitiful as he felt? He shook his head, throwing fine droplets of water around him.

"Hey, you're getting me wet," she squealed.

Ty looked at Michelle and smiled. His gaze dropped. Her shirt was plastered against her body, leaving nothing to his imagination. "It looks like you're wet already."

She looked down. Instantly she brought the towel in her hand up to cover her chest. "I'll go and change."

"You don't have to on my account," he called as she headed down the hall.

Michelle closed the door of her bedroom and leaned back against it. Had she lost her mind?

First she'd installed Ty in her home. Then she'd let him insist she sleep beside him and then she'd felt sorry for him and washed his hair. What was going to be next? Would he wiggle his finger and she would jump into bed with him?

She'd crossed that large black line of control she'd had over her life. Ty had ridden in and her brain had turned to mush. Grabbing a dry shirt out of her chest of drawers, she dragged off the wet one she wore and pulled on a dry one.

The glow in Ty's eyes had created an unfamiliar heat deep in her that felt so right. It had started a fire in her center that flowed out, ripple after ripple and made her feel alive. The man had a way of unlocking emotions she'd put away. Had her wanting things better left alone.

Taking a deep breath, she opened the door and went back into the kitchen. Ty was no longer there. Retracing her steps down the hall, she found the door to his room wide open. Ty lay on the bed sound asleep. What little activity he'd done had worn him out. He looked like a small boy, lying on his stomach, his face relaxed. It was a handsome face, all slants and planes. A golden tan covered his back. He was a man who spent time outdoors. The desire to touch him almost overwhelmed her. She wanted to caress that expanse of skin. Instead, she pulled the blanket she'd used during the night over him.

A lock of Ty's still damp hair had fallen over his forehead. Against her better judgment, but unable to resist, she pushed it back into place.

He shifted in his sleep, moaning as he did. Her heart went out to him. She wanted to take his aches away. He was so beat up that he couldn't even get into a hot bath to ease the soreness. Moving again, Ty wrapped his arms around a pillow and pulled it to his chest.

Michelle couldn't remember ever being jealous of an inanimate object before. She wished she could curl up next to his gorgeous body. But she couldn't.

Ty found Michelle sitting in the corner of the sofa in her living area. This room was off the kitchen but he'd not been in it before. Decorated in cheerful hues, like the rest of her place, the room also had a cozier feel. Quilted throws hung off the backs of the chairs and the lighting came from lamps instead of the harsher overhead lighting. Books lined one wall and the TV took a less prominent spot in the corner. She had it turned on and was watching an action movie that was about five years old. Even in her movie choices she continued to surprise him.

The sun was setting. Her face glowed in the last of the light filtering in from the window on the far wall. It was the type of light that a photographer dreamt of having when taking a picture of a subject. Michelle looked angelic. Ty couldn't help but admire her. She was pure beauty.

Michelle must have felt his eyes on her because she looked over the back of the sofa at him.

"Hey." He came further into the room.

"Hey, yourself. How are you feeling?" She twisted further towards him.

"Much better."

"Good."

He moved around the sofa. "Will you help me with this?" He held out his scrub shirt. "I can't seem to get it on by myself."

She stood and took it from him. Gathering the material up around the neck, she said, "Lean over."

He did so and she slipped the material over his head. Lifting his arms, she helped slide the shirt on and down. Her heat warmed him but not once did she touch him. He had no doubt that had been intentional. What was she scared of? There was something there between them, didn't she feel it too?

Michelle returned to the same spot on the sofa. He took the other end.

"You hungry? I didn't even wake you for lunch," she finally said.

"Yeah. I could eat."

She hopped up as if she was looking for an excuse to get away from him. "I'll fix you something."

He grabbed her wrist with his uninjured hand. She stopped and looked down at him. He pulled her down gently, this time closer to him. "You know what I'd really like to have?"

Michelle's eyes widened and she shook her head.

"A meat-lover's pizza. Why don't I buy you dinner?"

She pulled her hand from his. Her look of relief was almost laughable. "Did you think I was going to say something else?"

"No. No, I didn't. I'll call for the pizza. While we're waiting I'll give those bandages a look. You went to sleep so fast that I didn't have a chance to change them and I hated to wake you."

"I buy dinner if you want me to let you look at my stitches." He raised a challenging brow.

"You make it sound like I want to look at a tattoo on your butt."

He laughed. "Wouldn't you like to see it?"

Michelle rewarded him with an appalled look before she stood. "I'll call the pizza delivery place and get the supplies so I can give your arm and knee a look."

Ty listened as Michelle spoke into the phone and rattled around in the kitchen. It seemed like forever since he'd heard those sounds of domestic tranquility. It hadn't happened since he'd lived with his grandparents. His grandmother had made the same noises while his grandfather had sat in the den, reading the paper. They were the sounds of a home.

Bitter-sweet memories filled him. His grandparents had been both surprised and perplexed to see a teenager they'd barely known existed standing at their door. Despite that, they'd invited him in with open arms. It had been the first time he'd ever slept in the same place for over three months. The only time he'd known true stability.

They'd been so old when he'd arrived that he'd not only taken care of himself but often times them too. Somehow doing so had seemed to ease the pain he'd felt at not doing more for Joey. When they'd died within months of each other while he'd been in medical school he'd been devastated. What little foundation there had been in his world had crumbled. The last time he'd heard from his parents had been over three years ago. Who knew where they were now?

Michelle, returning with her hands full of supplies, interrupted his morose thoughts. "Interesting. A surgeon who is prepared," he said as she laid gauze, tape, and surgical scissors on the low table in front of them.

"It's just the usual first-aid type of stuff. Nothing special. Everyone has them."

"I don't."

She met his gaze. "And that would be because you don't stay in one place long enough to have a real home."

Michelle couldn't have made a more accurate shot if she'd punched him in a boxing match. She was right. He didn't, and he wanted it that way. Saw to it that he remained uninvolved.

"Remind me to stop by the drug store and buy a first-aid kit. How does that sound?"

"Smart. Now, let's have a look at your stitches first then I'll redo the gauze on your hand and knee before putting antibacterial ointment on those scrapes."

Michelle carefully cut the gauze and removed the pieces from his arm. She had a tender touch. A mother's touch. That was a completely random thought. If she ever became a mother it wouldn't involve him.

"All looks well. I'm going to just put a four-by-four over it but you're going to have to promise to keep it dry. No hair-washing on your own."

"Yes, ma'am. I'll let you do all my hair-washing."

She looked up at him with serious crystal-blue eyes. "You know making fun of the person who's taking care of you really isn't very smart. They might do something that hurts."

"I might be worried if it was someone else but I don't think you have a truly mean bone in your body. Under that armor of designer clothes, sexy shoes and all-business demeanor you're a softy. You've made a major mistake, Dr. Ross. You've let your guard down where I'm concerned."

Her pupils enlarged and she bit her upper lip. He could almost see the cogs turning in her brain. She looked so endearing and mystified he came close to leaning over and kissing her. She blinked and met his gaze again. The realization she'd been caught darkened her eyes.

Ty placed his hand over one of hers. "Hey, it's not the end of the world. I won't tell anyone, I promise."

She pursed her lips and that old resolve returned to her eyes. "Now you really are making fun of me. Let me see that hand."

He offered his bandaged hand. She took the same care with it as she had with the other but this time unwrapped it slowly. The last bit of gauze stuck to his raw skin. He winced.

Her head jerked up, eyes full of sympathy. She pressed her lips tightly together as she continued to work. When she pulled the last fragment free she said, "Oh, Ty, I'm so sorry. That has to hurt."

He looked at the red, angry area of his palm, which no longer had the top two layers of skin, then back at her. Michelle's eyes were luminous, heavy with tears. The woman did heart surgery and she was crying over him losing skin.

"Hey, don't cry, Michelle, ma belle. I'm okay." He brushed her cheek lightly with his uninjured hand.

She didn't say anything or look at him. Instead she picked up the ointment and started spreading it gently over his wound. Done, she covered it again. She didn't speak and neither did he.

After she'd rewrapped the gauze she said, "Hold this." He placed his fingertip where she indicated. Pulling a piece of tape off a roll, she secured the gauze.

"For me to rebandage your knee you're going to need to take off your pants and I need more gauze. While I'm gone, pull them down and make yourself decent using this blanket. I'll be right back."

"It's been a long time since a woman told me to pull

down my pants." He chuckled at the snort she gave as she left the room.

Michelle soon returned. "Put your heel on the table."

He did so and she started to work on removing the bandage, all business.

"You know, you have gorgeous hair," he said.

She gave him a quelling look.

"So you don't like to be complimented."

Her fingers continued to work with the same efficiency she did in the OR. "I didn't say that."

"Then you do like to be complimented."

She gave him a pointed look. "What I do know is that I'm used to my patients being sedated and I like it that way."

He laughed so hard he had to hold his sides because the pain was so great. "You are too much, Michelle."

"Would you be still and let me finish this?" Her lips quivered in her effort not to smile.

Minutes later she announced, "Good. There's no redness around the stitches." She began wrapping the new gauze into place.

Finished with the knee, she turned her back and let him pull his pants back up. Together they applied ointment to his other lacerations. Done, she gathered supplies. "I'm sorry I can't do something more for those bruises. They have to hurt."

"Maybe kiss them and make them better," he quipped.

"My mother isn't around." The words were as crisp as the leaves on the ground in fall.

He narrowed his eyes. "What does that have to do with it?"

"The only reason we would kiss is to make her happy."

Grabbing her, he jerked her against him. His hurt hand smarted but he didn't care. "I couldn't kiss you like I wanted to with your mother watching but I sure as hell can now."

He ran his fingers into her hair and, holding a mass of the sunny threads in his hand, he brought his mouth down to hers. Michelle would know this one was for her and not her mother.

Before Michelle could catch her breath, Ty's mouth seared hers. His tongue broke the seal of her lips and entered. He didn't ask permission but took. He demanded her attention, her acceptance. She held onto his shoulders, the only stable thing in her spinning world of pure pleasure.

Could she feel more alive? Need more? She was on fire.

Ty's tongue swept, demanded and conquered. His strong arms pulled her tighter until she leaned against him, almost sitting in his lap. Her fingers bit into the muscles of his forearm in an effort to find control.

It felt so good to be against him.

He pulled his mouth away just far enough to say, "Let go, Michelle. Experience it."

The dam burst on her control. She wrapped her arms around his neck and brought her mouth to his again. This time he didn't have to ask for entrance—she was there waiting with a welcome. She took all he gave and returned it. Blazing need pooled heavy and low in her. She writhed against him, pressing her breasts against his chest.

When he tried to pull away she moaned in resistance. She moved her hands up through his hair and directed his mouth to hers. His deep chuckle ripped through her as well as him, they were so close. Yet they weren't close enough. Time stood still as he took over the kiss.

The doorbell rang.

Ty's hands came down to rest on her waist. He gently pushed her away. "I do believe I might have created a monster."

Michelle stiffened and looked away, embarrassed and

angry at the same time. Could she have acted more desperate? Humiliated herself more?

The doorbell sounded again.

Ty placed a finger under her chin and lifted it so that she had to look into his eyes. "Hey, I'm not complaining. Desire is the most perfect form of flattery. And I'm definitely flattered."

She gave him a wry smile.

He dropped a quick kiss on her lips. "I'll get the pizza."

She and Ty decided to eat on the floor in the living room and watch a movie. They found that they were both big fans of action adventure films. She would never have guessed when he'd come into her OR that day that she would have ever had anything in common with Ty. He continued to dumbfound her. By just riding into town he'd tipped her ordered world sideways. Somehow he'd added an excitement to it that she hadn't even known had been missing.

With the movie credits rolling, she pulled herself up off the floor and started to gather the plates and pizza box.

"Do you always have to clean up? Have everything just so?"

She looked down to where Ty still sat with his back against the sofa.

"Leave it. You'd be amazed at how freeing it is. Bet you can't do it."

She dropped the empty box onto the table with a thud and turned to walk away. "Goodnight."

"I didn't mean to make you mad." He sounded truly apologetic.

"It does get old when you're always making snide remarks about how I live, dress, act."

"Hey…" Ty made an effort to stand and groaned in the process.

Unable to help herself, Michelle rushed to him. "What's wrong?"

"I'm just stiff from sitting so long. How about giving me a hand?" He reached his hand towards her.

If she touched him again, what would happen? She'd made a point to keep distance between them as they'd watched the movie she'd still been acutely aware of him the entire time. Particularly after their hot unforgettable kiss earlier. Fear controlled her. She was afraid she could go into his arms far too easily, into his bed. And why shouldn't she? He'd be gone soon. She'd be able to return to her settled life. But could she keep her heart uninvolved? She knew what losing someone did to a person. Would it be worth it?

"It isn't a commitment for life. I just need a tug up."

The man was perceptive. He didn't miss much about her or people in general. That was a trait to be admired.

"Come on, Michelle, ma belle," Ty sang, "live a little. Help a man out."

His grin, as always, was infectious.

Michelle put out her hand and his firm, large one encircled hers. It was emblematic of what he was doing to her life. Blanketing it, binding her more securely to him.

She stepped back on one foot and pulled. Ty, in a lithe movement that made her suspect that he might have been faking his aches and pains, came to his feet. As he moved upwards she leaned further back. When she started to stumble his grip became stronger. He pulled her forward against his solid body, his arm circled her waist and held her firmly in place.

Ty's eyes captured and held her attention. His mouth hovered inches from hers. She wanted to lean forward and touch them with her own, feel them pressed against hers again. Swallowing, she said, "You made up needing help."

"Truthfully, I didn't but it worked out well anyway."

His mouth lowered, taking hers gently, testing. This time he was asking.

Her cellphone sitting on the table rang and rattled against the wood.

"You're not on call. It'll keep," Ty whispered against her ear, before he kissed the sweet spot behind it.

She wanted to do as he'd asked but she couldn't throw away ingrained habits so easily, despite being on the road to heaven.

"I can't." She stepped away and Ty let her go.

"I know. It's who you are."

Michelle picked up the cellphone and answered. She listened, suddenly feeling sick. "I'll be right there."

Tears hit her cheeks before she could get them under control.

Ty put his hands on her shoulders. "What's wrong?"

"My mom's in the hospital. She collapsed. Her neighbor found her. I forgot to call," she said frankly.

"Because of me."

Michelle didn't answer. "I have to go." She headed towards her room for her shoes.

"I'm going with you."

She stopped and looked at Ty. "No, you need to stay here and rest. You look like a postcard for a hospital stay yourself. Being black and blue."

"If I were a man with less self-esteem I might be devastated by that comment. I'm going with you."

"You don't—"

"I said I'm going."

She'd been alone with her mother's illness for so long that she couldn't imagine what it would be like to have someone along for support. It sounded nice, really nice. "Okay, but I don't know how long I'll be."

"It doesn't matter. I'll stay as long as you do."

"If you start hurting you're getting a taxi back here. I don't need two people in the hospital to care for."

"Yes, ma'am."

She knew that tone well by now. Ty would do as he pleased, no matter what she said.

"Michelle."

She looked at him. "Yes."

"Don't think what was happening here is over."

Heat zipped through her, carrying anxiety, apprehension and the sweet thrill of anticipation. Ty wanted her. Not only now but later.

CHAPTER SIX

TY WAS GLAD to see Mrs. Ross settled in a room and comfortable. Her blood count had dipped, making her feel lightheaded and causing her to fall. With a blood transfusion and a couple of days' stay in the hospital, she'd be home again.

Michelle had stress written all over her face. Was this the same self-assured woman Ty was beginning to know so well? Her mother's illness was taking its toll. Her breakdown in the OR and the over-the-top fear she'd experienced when she'd been called about her mother said her emotions were tissue-paper thin. She'd been carrying the load of worry by herself for far too long.

At least he was here for her now. He hadn't been for Joey. That pure, raw panic in Michelle's eyes had reached deep in him, to the place where he didn't want to return.

Ty looked at the mother and daughter as they spoke quietly. Where it had once been a strong woman and a weaker one, now all Ty saw was two fragile women who loved each other. Even though he wasn't completely comfortable with how involved in Michelle's life he had become he would support her to the best of his ability until it was time for him to leave.

"You two need to go home. I'm all right. The nurses will take good care of me tonight," Mrs. Ross said, looking past Michelle to where he sat.

"Mother, I don't want to leave you in here alone," Michelle said.

In a stronger voice Mrs. Ross said, "Ty, please see that Michelle gets home safely. She's tired and you don't look much better. You shouldn't have come anyway with all those injuries." She looked back at her daughter. "I'll go to sleep as soon as you are both gone."

"Mom—"

"No argument. Ty, take care of her."

"Yes, ma'am." He went to stand beside Michelle's chair. "Come on. We'll come back first thing in the morning." He took her elbow with his uninjured hand and urged her to stand.

Michelle leaned over and kissed her mother. "I'll see you in the morning."

"I'll be here." Her mother gave her a weak smile. "Thanks, Ty."

He nodded. In the parking lot he said, "Let me have your keys. You're too done in to drive."

"You drive a motorcycle." Michelle yawned wide and long.

"I assure you I remember how to drive a car."

Michelle handed over the keys without further argument. Ty helped her into the passenger side of the car and closed the door. She was dead on her feet. He'd had induced sleep the night before while she'd been up checking on him every hour or so. He didn't remember every time she had, but as conscientious as she was he knew she'd done it. If he didn't miss his guess he'd say she'd not slept any today either.

As a surgeon part of her job was to have the stamina to work long hours but that wasn't when you were emotionally involved. Worry over her mother had drained her.

Before he'd pulled out of the lot, Michelle's head was bobbing. "Put your head on my shoulder."

She shook her head. "You're bruised."

"I'm a big boy, I can handle it."

She didn't fight him or argue further. Leaning her head against him, she was resting peacefully seconds later. There was something right about having her under his care. It made him think of what-ifs. But he didn't do long term. Didn't stay in one place. Guilt ate at him. He'd let Joey down. Would end up letting Michelle down also.

It was better not to get involved. But on some level wasn't he already?

Michelle woke to Ty calling her name. What a wonderful way to come out of sleep.

"We're home. I wouldn't have woken you and just carried you into the house but my hand and arm…"

"Hey, it's the thought that counts. I can walk."

"Thanks for letting my ego down easy."

She went in ahead of him. "I'll get your medicine."

Ty stepped to the kitchen counter to stand beside her. He took the prescription bottle out of her hand and put it down. He cupped her cheek with his good hand. "I can take care of myself. You've looked after everyone but yourself today. Go and get into bed."

Michelle blinked slowly with a drowsy look that made him think of tangled sheets and her beneath him. She had no idea of the power she was gaining over him. Thankfully she didn't argue, which told him just how worn out she was.

"Goodnight," she mumbled as she walked off.

Ty groaned. He needed to take something that would make him sleep because every fiber in him wanted to follow right behind her and straight into her bed. But he wouldn't take the medicine. He wanted to be alert if Michelle needed him during the night.

After securing the condo for the night, he headed down

the hall towards his room. As he was entering, a sound of glass breaking came from Michelle's room.

Ty went to her door, which was slightly open. "Michelle, is everything all right?"

A muffle sound was all the response he received.

He nudged the door wider. "Michelle, are you hurt?"

"I…need your help," came from the direction of what had to be the bathroom. Ty stalked across the room and didn't hesitate to enter the bathroom.

Tears ran down Michelle's face. She sat on the edge of the tub with a towel haphazardly wrapped around her, leaving more skin exposed than covered. If she hadn't looked so distraught he would have tugged on that towel and finished what they had started earlier in the evening.

Instead, he saw shattered glass surrounding her feet and some type of pink-colored liquid on the floor. Michelle held her hand in her lap. A finger dripped blood.

"I don't know what's wrong with me," she sobbed.

Ty's heart contracted. An emotionally brittle Michelle tore at his soul.

Still wearing his shoes, he stepped further into the bathroom and snatched a hand towel off a hook. Lifting Michelle's injured hand, he wrapped the towel around it. He ignored his injuries that screamed against the pressure as he scooped her up into his arms.

She didn't resist, leaning her head on his shoulder. So frayed, she didn't comment on his wounds either.

He laid her on the bed. "Stay put. I'll get something for that finger."

She rolled away from him and pulled her knees up to her chest. The towel around her body slipped upwards, barely covering her bottom. Ty turned away and made his way to the kitchen to find the first-aid supplies she'd used on him earlier in the day. Locating them in a small drawer, he took out what he thought he'd need. By the amount of blood he'd seen, it looked as if she might need stitches.

Returning to her room, he found Michelle still curled on the bed. She looked so lost and pitiful. This was no longer the self-assured, in-control, sharp-tongued woman he knew from the OR. Michelle had morphed into a scared, exhausted and heartbroken daughter with an ill mother. The ice queen had turned human.

His chest tightened. All he wanted to do was to gather her up and hold her tight, reassuring her that all would be well. But if he did, could he stop there?

She needed someone to care for her. To help her carry her burdens. To stand beside her when she required help. Could he be that person? His past said no. But he was here now. He would take care of her while he was here.

Ty sat on the edge of the bed. "Michelle, you're going to have to roll over and let me see your finger. We need to get it covered or you'll get blood all over the bedspread." He reached out to touch her shoulder but only let it hover, unable to trust himself if he came in contact with the creamy skin. He rested his hand on the bed. "Come on, ma belle, let me see your finger."

Michelle rolled but remained in the same fetal position. She flopped her hand out into his lap. Ty undid the towel and was pleased to see that the cut wasn't as extensive as he'd expected. Using the wet cloth he'd brought from the kitchen, he cleaned the blood away. A sticking-plaster would do.

She watched him work with blank eyes. She didn't even wince when he touched the cut with the cloth. Her detachment worried him. Had she become so despondent that she'd given up?

As he finished applying the dressing he smiled at her and said, "You know, at this rate the two of us aren't going to generate much trust in our patients. We both look like accidents waiting to happen."

He was pleased to see a slight smile form on her lips. He liked it. She didn't do it often enough.

"I'm going to clean up the mess in the bathroom. While I'm doing that why don't you put on a nightgown and get into bed? You'll feel better after a good night's rest."

Not waiting for her answer, he took the first-aid supplies back to the kitchen and found the broom and dustpan. When he returned Michelle was asleep but still covered in only the towel and lying on top of the spread.

Putting the broom and dustpan in the bathroom, he came back and pulled the spread away on the opposite side of the bed from Michelle. Circling around to her side again, he lifted her. She snuggled against him, warm and perfect. She was very appealing with her hair disheveled and so much smooth skin showing. Most troubling of all was that she smelled wonderful. Like springtime flowers and rain.

Ty placed her on the sheet and gently pulled the towel from her with a growl of remorse and a straining of his manhood. Reminding himself that at this time she was more patient than lover, he resisted the urge to linger and look his fill. With a jerk of the covers he pulled the top sheet and spread up over Michelle's shoulders.

After turning the bedside table lamp on and the overhead light off, he headed to the bathroom to clean up. Minutes later he had what he assumed was bath oil removed from the floor. The smell was strong but it reminded him of the sleeping woman who so tempted him in the bed just a few feet away. With a sharp note to keep his mind on the job, he went back to sweeping.

This clean-up job was the most domestic thing he'd done in years. In fact, the last few days had been most unusual. Eating in a kitchen. Sleeping in a real home. Being a part of someone's life. For once in a long time he wished for more. These types of thoughts wouldn't lead to anything positive. He'd already learned more than once that he couldn't take a chance on having those feelings. It was too easy for it all to be gone. It wasn't worth the pain.

Replacing the broom and dustpan, he threw the towels he'd used to clean up the oil into the washer. He'd check on Michelle and head to bed.

Unable to resist touching her and making the excuse that she might have a fever, he pushed a ribbon of hair away from her face. He was pleased to find that her skin was cool. Satisfied she wasn't sick but unsatisfied where his body was concerned, he reached over and turned out the lamp.

"Ty."

"Yes, ma belle?"

"Would you hold me?" The words came out as if she was bone weary.

He stood shock still. Could he? Could he not?

"I'm so cold inside."

He'd hold her until she went back to sleep. Surely he could muster that much self-control over his basic instincts and help her through this time. But she was naked.

Breathing deeply and kicking off his shoes, he slid under the covers and onto his side. He ran his unbandaged arm under her neck and the other circled her waist. This time he was grateful that a bandage covered most of his hand. If he been able to feel her skin against his palm there would have been no way to control his desires. Michelle snuggled up against him and with a deep sigh stilled. He gritted his teeth and tried to think about taking a bath in ice water. Seconds later her even breathing told him she was asleep again.

Would she even know she'd asked him into her bed tomorrow? Or what he'd suffered to be here?

His fingertips brushed her skin. It felt warm and silky smooth. He wanted to explore more of her. With a groan, he shifted. Even the loose pants of his scrubs felt tight. With great effort he pushed the fact that she was naked out of his mind, or at least tried to. It was impossible. His body throbbed with lust, despite his best efforts to convince it otherwise.

Ty rubbed his cheek against her soft hair. Breathing in the floral scent of her bath oil, which was as classy as Michelle, he looked off into the dark. He begged for sleep to ease the agony, confident it would never come. The night would be a long one.

Michelle shifted to find a wall of warmth preventing her from totally rolling over. She snuggled closer, her face padded against the musk of heated skin. Wanting more, she put an arm over it and aligned herself.

"Michelle. Stop."

A dark rumble above her head jerked her to reality. She held her breath.

"Let go, Michelle, so I can move."

She didn't. She didn't want to. Didn't want Ty to move.

Ty felt so good against her. She wanted more. All of him. Her hand rested partly on material and partly on skin. She nudged what had to be his scrub shirt upwards until her hand found heated skin.

"Mmm." Her fingertips flowed over the skin, feeling it ripple.

A groan of deep agony warned, "Michelle, wake up."

"I don't want to. This is a nice dream," she mumbled as she traced the line of his last rib. "It feels good. I want to feel good."

The rush of air being forcefully sucked in came from above. "If you keep that up it won't be a dream but reality."

"Okay," she said, pushing the material further out of the way.

He winced.

Had she lost her mind? She was coming on to a man who had been in an accident. He was hurt, sore. She had reached a new low in the need department. But what would be so wrong with them making each other feel good for just a little while? Ty wanted her. He'd made that clear.

Looking up, she found his heavy-lidded eyes focused on her.

"I'm sorry. I'm hurting you." She moved away.

"Hey, come back here. This is the kind of pain I like." His voice was a low gravel tone laced with desire that made her nerve endings sing.

Running her hand further under his shirt, she trailed the flat of her hand across the contours of his chest, following every dip and curve. He didn't move, letting her explore to her heart's content. The palm of her hand caressed and came to rest low on his belly. She leaned over and kissed the spot where her hand had been.

Ty hissed in response, "Michelle, if you go much further there'll be no stopping."

"I'm not a child. I know what I'm doing. Yes. I want this. I want to feel good, alive."

Ty's hands gripped her under her arms and pulled her up until his lips almost touched hers. "Aw, ma belle, I'm just the man for the job."

His mouth took hers in a sweeping kiss, like none she'd ever experienced. His tongue demanded entrance and she gave it. He savored and devoured, then turned playful again.

Her breasts tingled, tightened as her nipples hardened, anticipating Ty's touch.

His hands roamed with complete freedom along her sides and over her bare bottom. He lifted her, bringing her closer. She felt the ridge of his arousal against her stomach. A giddy feeling rippled through her. She'd made Ty want her in the most elemental way. The man who charmed all the women and could have anyone wanted her. *Her.*

Michelle pushed at his shirt again. She wore no clothes but he was still dressed. She wanted her skin against his. Wanted all of him. Wanted, needed to be touched, tasted and be taken. Whatever it took to forget her responsibilities. To live for herself for once.

"Off." He let her go and she rolled away. He raised his chest inches from the mattress and she helped him remove his shirt.

His arms circled her again and her breasts came to rest against his chest. She shifted, trying to get closer. His heat and need flowed through her. With a grunt that reminded her that he was hurt, he rolled her onto her back.

"Ty, you're hurt—"

"Shut up," he said softly. His mouth captured hers. Slowly, far too slowly his hands moved towards her breasts. They ached for his touch. Her nipples beaded, rose and awaited his consideration.

One hand came to lie wide and heavy on her middle. He made small tantalizing circles along her skin, which sent ripples of desire dancing through her. She sucked in a breath, held it as his fingertips worked magic.

This was living. Something she'd put on hold for far too long. And even if it was just for tonight, she would grasp this feeling with both hands.

Ty finally cupped a straining breast and her hips flexed. He lifted the weight of her breast and ran a fingertip around the tip. She throbbed in her center, burned with need. She opened her eyes to find Ty watching her. His eyes had turned the dark green of a forest in summer. They bored into hers.

He continued to tease her breast as he whispered, "There's nothing icy about you. You are pure molten lava for me. Ma belle."

His mouth dipped to favor a nipple.

Her hips came off the bed and her eyes closed as she sailed away on a tide of pure pleasure.

His mouth released her. When he pulled away she let out a sound of disappointment, begging for more. If he didn't touch her...

Ty didn't disappoint. Moving to the other breast, he took it into his mouth. He tormented and teased by circling his tongue around her pebbled tip. She throbbed with a craving that only Ty could satisfy. His attention brought white-hot heat to where she wanted him most.

His lips came back to hers, before departing again to leave small kisses along her jaw line. He pushed her hair away and kissed the sweet dip behind her ear. She shivered and brought her legs up to circle his hips.

Ty broke her grip and shimmied down her body, leaving wet kisses as he went. She clawed at his shoulders to stop him.

"Oh, no, here you don't run the show. We share. Right now it's my turn," Ty growled.

"I want—"

"I know you do. I do too. But not yet. I must enjoy you some more."

Ty kissed her belly, orbited her bellybutton with his tongue. She flinched and groaned.

"So responsive. So hot for me," Ty rasped, his voice rich with approval.

He continued to place kisses over her skin, across the ridge of her hip bones and lower. Michelle's fingers found his hair and played with it, letting it fall between her fin-

gers. Watching as a curl caressed her fingertip. It was as
wonderful as she had imagined it to be.

One of Ty's hands found her calf and slowly slid up to
her knee. His finger caressed the underside until she could
stand it no longer and pulled way.

The small rumble in his chest said that had been his
plan. She opened for him and he pressed his advantage.
His talented and capable fingers traveled along the length
of the inside of her thigh, teased and moved down to her
knee again.

Michelle whimpered with disappointment. She wasn't
going to be able to take much more. Then his fingers started
their slow, excruciatingly magnificent travel upwards once
more. He did it again and again, each time stopping just a
little closer to her begging center.

Her hands clawed at the sheets. She'd become nothing
but a mass of wonton, beseeching need. He was driving
her beyond reason.

Finally, Ty's finger touched her center and her hips
arched off the bed.

"Easy. Soon. Very soon." His finger entered her waiting
heat and she came unglued, bursting with release. His body
covered hers and their lips met. "That was a beautiful thing
to behold, ma belle, but we're not finished."

Ty pushed up and away from her as if any pain or soreness he might have felt was forgotten. He headed out the
door as if on a mission. Michelle curled into the bed and
enjoyed the lovely waves of pleasure that Ty had left behind. Seconds later, he returned with a packet of protection.
She watched as he peeled out of his pants and underwear
at the same time.

There was nothing bashful about this man as he stood
proudly before her, all wild hair, expansive chest, flat
stomach, slim hips and strong thighs. The most obvious

was his desire for her standing tall and ready. Michelle couldn't take her eyes off him. He was the Greek god of her dreams.

Ty took care of protecting them. The bed dipped as he rejoined her. "There's no going back from here, Michelle. You say the word and I'll leave," he said quietly but with meaning.

She wrapped her arms around his neck and pulled him to her. He lowered and surrounded her. With a sigh, she accepted his weight. For once she wasn't afraid to be out of control. To have someone take the lead.

He kissed her deep and long before his hands found her breasts and gave them the attention they longed for. He shifted so that she cradled him between her legs. His manhood rested at her entrance.

"Look at me," he growled. "I want to see that passion you try so hard to hide when I enter you."

Her eyes flickered up to meet his. As if he could stand it no longer, he buried himself deep in her. Ty leaned down and breathed into her ear, "Heaven, ma belle."

He pulled back then pushed forward again. Michelle flexed to meet him, taking him completely. Ty increased the pace. She joined him. As they moved faster, she climbed higher. Reaching her peak, she exploded into beautiful waves of perfect bliss. With the sound of her name drifting off his lips and a final thrust, Ty found his completion. His weight covered her but she offered no complaint.

Some time later, Michelle lay with her head on Ty's stomach as he played with her hair. She lifted his hand with the bandage and kissed each fingertip. "You are right. We are a pair."

"How's that?"

"You're all banged up and even I have an injury. We

won't inspire much confidence as doctors." She held up her finger and giggled. She couldn't remember the last time she'd truly giggled. Ty brought that out in her. She felt wonderful.

"I'll kiss yours if you'll kiss mine."

She looked up at him. He had a wicked grin on his face.

"That sounds like a fine idea. I get to go first." She rolled over and placed a kiss just below his waist and moved downwards. She fully expected to have another mind-blowing, body-sedating and deliciously satisfying experience this time around as well.

Ty woke to the afternoon sun shining into the room. Michelle's leg lay over one of his. Even in her sleep she tried to dominate. Earlier, he'd let her and had more than enjoyed it. Her hand rested on one of his shoulders and she had a handful of his hair intertwined in her fingers. Her head had found a bed in the crook of the other shoulder.

He was sore and stiff from the motorcycle accident and the events of the night before had not improved that but he wouldn't have missed having the responsive and tender Michelle in his arms for anything. It felt right to have her there. As if she belonged. It had been a long time since anyone had belonged to him.

They'd slept, made love and slept again. Michelle had gotten up long enough to call and check on her mother. After receiving a favorable report, she'd returned to him. Their lovemaking had been slow and gentle the next time as if they'd both wanted it to be special.

Michelle stirred beside him and he hugged her close. It was nice, really nice. Could he do this every day? Looking down at her face, he wished he could. The question was did he know how? He had no experience at staying in one place or having someone depend on him.

His heart thumped hard against his chest. What was happening? This feeling was foreign to him. He'd no intention of caring, didn't want to take the chance. Had fought it for years. Was he falling for Michelle? Had it already happened?

She twisted in his arms and her hand rubbed his cheek. "You need a shave."

"You weren't complaining about it a while ago."

"I guess I wasn't," she said softly. "Ty, I want to thank you."

What? The world as he knew it had made a one-eighty turn and she was thanking him for sex. Had he been used? He sure felt like it.

"I appreciate…this…all you've done," she went on, oblivious to the fact she was stabbing him in the heart.

Ty sat up. "Hell, Michelle, that wasn't sympathy sex. There's more than that between us. I know you want people to believe you're a cold fish, but I know better."

He disentangled himself from her, pushed the sheet away and stood.

Michelle opened her mouth as if to speak.

"Stop there, Michelle. You've already said enough."

She sat up, pulling the sheet over her breasts. "Where's this coming from? You don't take anything seriously. You're planning to leave soon."

"Sure I do. I was serious last night. Plenty serious about you."

"You can't be, we don't even have anything in common."

"It sure seemed like we had plenty in common last night and a number of times after that."

"Relationships are made up of more than sex."

"So all that has happened between us you sum up as just being sex?"

She gasped.

"Exactly. It does sound cold and one-sided."

He snatched up his clothes and headed for the other bedroom. After calling a taxi, he washed up the best he could and was waiting on the curb when his ride arrived.

CHAPTER SEVEN

THE NEXT WEEK was the longest and most difficult of any Michelle had experience since her father had passed away. She'd never felt more alone.

Her mother had been released from the hospital and was doing well. She asked about Ty often but Michelle dodged her questions. How could she tell her mother what had happen between her and Ty?

Work was the worst. She saw Ty but then really didn't. To her great surprise he was no longer assigned to her OR. They might pass at the scrub sink or at the nurses' station but they had become strangers. For two people to have shared such closeness, they were a world apart now.

She would never have thought she would miss Ty so much. He'd gotten under her skin. Had become part of her life in such a short time.

"Dr. Ross, is everything okay with you?" Jane, her surgical nurse, asked after one of their cases.

"Yes, why?" She didn't dare admit that she was pining for Ty.

"You just haven't been yourself the last week or so. I'm… concerned about you."

Michelle stopped what she was doing and looked at Jane. "You've never asked me anything personal before so why now?"

"I don't know. You seemed to have changed somehow. Like you're giving me a chance to ask." She hesitated then said, "I know what's said about you but I also know you care about the patients above all else, even to your own detriment. I see it in the way you worry over them. Don't let what some of the nurses say get to you. There are those of us who know differently."

Michelle was speechless. She and Jane had worked together for years and this was the first time Michelle had ever heard anything like this from her. "Thank you, Jane. That means a lot to me."

The woman gave Michelle a reassuring smile.

A few days later, Michelle overheard a group of the nurses talking about going to Buster's to hear the surgeons' band play.

Taking a breath, she asked, "Do you mind…uh…if I join you?"

The shock on the nurses' faces would have been comical if not for the fact it was so sad that she had chosen to be so remote that she received that type of reaction.

Jane stepped forward, "We'll save you a place at the table."

The other nurses murmured their agreement.

"Thank you. I'd like that." She gave them all a sincere smile as they headed toward the locker room.

"Jane," Michelle said.

The nurse stopped and turned back to Michelle with a questioning look on her face.

"May I ask you something?"

"Sure."

"I saw the looks on the others' faces just now. Have I really been that bad?"

"Yeah, I guess you have. You're a great surgeon but not

very personable." Jane reached out and placed a hand on Michelle's arm. "But I think that's changing."

Michelle gave her a weak smile. "Thanks, Jane."

She gave Michelle a reassuring smile. "I'll see you this evening."

A couple of hours later Michelle groaned when she looked at the growing pile of clothing on her bed. Since when did she have such an issue with dressing? She'd always laid out her outfit for the next day, had everything organized. She looked at the rows of suits and dresses hanging in the closet in perfect order. For some reason she wanted to shake things up a bit. Wanted to live a little differently. Wanted Ty's attention again.

She'd hurt his feelings unintentionally. Their time together had been earth-shattering for her. If she let herself care he'd break her heart, she had no doubt about that. Nothing about Ty said permanence. No stability. She had to have that. There was her mother to consider. Her job. Even if she wanted to she couldn't pick up and follow him if he asked her to, which he hadn't. Her practical side couldn't help but remember that he was only here for a few more weeks.

Right now he wouldn't even have a conversation with her. Their time in bed together had been wonderful, but she found she yearned for their discussions. His sharp wit when they disagreed. His smiles, making her laugh, getting her to have a different perspective on things. She missed their friendship.

Wow. They'd had a friendship. She'd not had a real friend in years. Someone who knew what was going on in her life. She'd actually confided in Ty. That was something she'd even had difficulty doing with her mother.

Maybe tonight he'd speak to her. See that she was trying to say she was sorry, attempting to make a change. Maybe they could get back on a better footing. What she wanted was for them to at least be friends.

Running out of time, she settled on a pair of designer jeans. She'd not worn them for months and was pleased to discover they fit perfectly. After adding a red short-sleeved shirt and red patent heels, she was pleased with the effect. When was the last time she'd spent this much time fussing over what she wore? She usually did it with confidence and very little thought. Had she ever dressed to get the attention of a man before? She took longer than usual with her make-up and hair. After adding some swinging earrings and jingly bracelets, she was ready. She looked into the mirror and smiled. Surely Ty would notice her.

With an unfamiliar nervous flutter in her belly, she picked up her keys and headed out the door. By the time she reached Buster's much of her confidence had waned. She drove an extra trip around the block in an effort to fortify herself.

What if Jane and the others didn't talk to her? What if she had to sit at a table alone? Worse, what if Ty was there with a date?

For heaven's sake, when had she become so insecure? When Ty had shown up.

She was a well-respected heart surgeon in a large metropolitan hospital. She'd been taking care of herself, her mother and patients for years, so why was she having such a difficult time going into a public place and having a drink? Because she was scared.

She pulled into the first parking spot open. Enough of that.

Entering Buster's, her eyes needed to adjust to the dim lighting. She stood to the side of the doorway, pushing away the urge to turn and run. Just as she'd made up her mind to do so, Jane appeared beside her.

"Hey, Dr. Ross. I'm glad you came. We have a table right up front. Been saving you a seat."

"Hi Thanks." Michelle followed Jane through the crowd to the table.

Six other OR nurses Michelle recognized were already there.

"Hey, everyone. Dr. Ross made it," Jane announced.

Each said hi and gave Michelle unsure smiles. They were obviously uncomfortable about sharing their table with the ice queen. She'd have to work on changing that. "Hello. Please call me Michelle."

That request brought on jaw-dropping looks from almost everyone. Jane took one of the vacant chairs and Michelle squeezed into another. The serving girl wearing short shorts and a tight T-shirt came by and asked for their drink order.

Michelle looked around but didn't see Ty. Lauren, one of the nurses sitting on the other side of her, leaned over and said, "I've been wanting to ask you where you buy your clothes."

A ripple of pleasure went through Michelle at the un- expected question. The others around the table leaned in closer to hear her answer. She smiled at them all. "I shop at a number of places. But I really like this particular bou- tique over in Winston-Salem."

"You'll have to give us directions. You always look so put together."

"Thank you." She gave them a bright smile.

"Maybe we could plan a girls' day out and you could show us where it is," Jane suggested.

Girls' day? That sounded kind of nice. "Sure," Michelle said.

"Then let's plan it for some time soon," the nurse across the table said.

Michelle smiled. "Okay."

The band started filing onto the tiny stage area in the back of the room and to the right of them. Michelle was acquainted with all the band members but the one who had her complete attention was Ty.

He wore his usual jeans and T-shirt that she'd come to recognize as his favorite clothing, even though she'd only seen him briefly and even then in scrubs in the last few weeks. His attire tonight suited him. Even in dress, they were opposites.

Ty stood to the side of the leader of the band and focused on tuning his guitar. Minutes later the band broke into their first song. It was an upbeat rock-and-roll number that everyone was familiar with. The crowd went wild.

They moved from that song right into the next. The band was quite good. Ty had a real flair for the dramatic on the guitar, which wasn't unexpected. His playing was an extension of his personality. The crowd showed their appreciation a number of times and most of the women couldn't keep their eyes off him.

The band was well into the third number when Ty scanned the crowd. Michelle saw the instant he became aware of her. His gaze had gone past her and quickly returned. His look didn't waver from where she sat. She smiled. Good. He'd been shocked to see her. For once, he was the one off balance.

For a moment his fingers hesitated on the strings of the guitar. Seconds later his attention was forced to return to the number he played. During the rest of the set, his eyes continued to drift her direction.

After one of the times Ty had stared at her, she glanced at Jane to find her watching her. Jane leaned over and said into Michelle's ear, "Ty sure is interested in someone at our table."

She shrugged. "I guess so."

* * *

Michelle made her way to the restroom during the band's break. Exiting the restroom, she stopped short when she saw Ty standing with his back against the wall, hands in his pockets and one foot over the other. He gave her a level look.

"Slumming tonight, Michelle?"

Her heart constricted. She might have deserved the shot but that didn't mean she liked hearing it. "You invited me. Remember?"

"That was weeks ago."

She shrugged a shoulder. "So I was a little late showing up." He wasn't going to make this easy. "The band is good. You're good."

He lips tightened and he nodded, not taking his eyes off her, as if he was having to plan his response.

She waited, not sure what would happen next or even what she wanted.

"Why are you here, Michelle?"

Apparently he wanted her to spell it out.

A woman came down the hall heading in their direction.

Michelle glanced at her, unsure about baring her heart in front of a stranger.

"Come with me." Ty grabbed her hand and pull her further down the hall.

"Where're we going?"

He paused and pinned her with a look. "For once, just let me lead."

They stopped in front of a door. He knocked. There was no answer so he opened it, pulled her in. It was an office. A lone small lamp burn on the desk. Ty closed the door behind them.

"I'll ask it again. Why're you here, Michelle?"

"Don't you know?"

"Maybe. But I want you to tell me."

She took a deep breath. Ty's gaze slipped down to her chest and quickly returned to her eyes. At least he still found her desirable. That was a positive sign.

"I'm sorry I hurt you. I didn't mean to. Please forgive me."

Ty stood looking at her long enough that she feared he would reject her.

"I shouldn't let you off so easily." Suddenly he closed the few steps that were between them. He pressed her against the back of the door with his body while his hands burrowed though her loose hair. His lips swooped down to capture hers.

With a moan she circled his waist with her arms and pulled him closer. Ty didn't have to request entrance into her mouth, she offered it. Michelle grabbed the whirling and unfurling sensations flowing through her and hung on for the ride, having no idea how much she'd missed Ty until that moment.

"Mmm," she moaned.

"Missed me, did you?" Ty said as he left kisses on her nose and eyes.

"Maybe a little."

He chuckled and pressed his hips into her. "I missed you just a little too, Michelle, ma belle."

Ty lips took hers again, but this time the kiss was more restrained, making her beg for more.

There was a knock at the door. "Hey, Ty, you in there? We're on in five."

"I'll be right there," Ty called, then leaned his forehead against hers.

The sound of their panting filled the small area.

"I've got to step away from you right now or I won't be presentable in public."

It was empowering to know she had such an effect on Ty. It was an intoxicating feeling.

He stepped back, letting his hands caress her cheeks as he did. He moved to stand beside the desk well out of her touching distance. Her hands itched to have him close again.

His eyes started at the top of her head and moved slowly down her to stop at her shoes. "You sure look incredibly sexy tonight. I particularly love those hot red shoes. I hope all that effort was for my benefit."

"Could be I came to see one of the other band members play."

He growled. "Even if you did, you'll be leaving with me."

Was he jealous? "Nice to know that your ego hasn't deflated any over the last few weeks."

"You might be surprised how easy it is to damage my ego."

Michelle's heart skipped a beat. Was she really that important to him?

"I'll leave with whoever I wish."

In two quick steps Ty had her in his arms again. "I don't think so," he said before his lips met hers. When he pulled away his mouth hovered just above hers. "I'll tell you what, you promise I'm the only person you'll leave with and I'll buy you a burger after the last set. Maybe tell you which table Buster dedicated to your father."

Her eyes widened. "What?"

"You heard me. We'll talk about it over that burger." He gave her a quick kiss. "Now I've got to go."

Michelle moved so Ty could open the door. He allowed her to leave ahead of him. As they walked down the hall, Jane approached them. She looked from Michelle to Ty and back again. A large grin formed on her face. "Hello, Ty, Michelle."

"Hey, Jane," Ty said as they passed her.

"Ty," Jane called above the sounds of the band warming up.

"Yeah?"

"You might want to wipe that red lipstick off before you go on stage."

Michelle had no doubt that her face had turned the same color as her lips.

He grinned and rubbed the back of his hand across his lips. "Thanks, Jane. Michelle attacked me."

Michelle held her head high and kept moving, grateful for the low light. For once she didn't care who knew her business. Ty was at least speaking to her.

Ty had hardly been able to believe his eyes when he'd seen Michelle in the audience. He'd done a true double-take. He hadn't had to wonder if she'd come to see him—it was as good as written all over her face. Her eyes were for him only.

He'd worked his way to her table after the first set to find her not there. Without asking, Jane had pointed him in the direction of the restroom. He'd tried to look casual as he'd waited for Michelle to come out, but his insides had been churning. Thinking of little else but wanting Michelle and remembering those extraordinary hours they'd spent together had made the last two weeks apart horrible.

He wanted her to regret treating what had been the hottest night of passion he'd ever experienced as if he'd been there only to help her through a bad time. But to be fair, he hadn't led her to believe that their relationship would be anything but a casual thing, only lasting until he left. He hadn't changed his mind. But at least this way she wouldn't expect something more, something he couldn't give.

When Michelle had finally emerged from the ladies room he'd wavered between relief and insecurity. Would she be glad to see him?

He'd meant to be cool, to act as if her being there hadn't affected him. It had worked for a little while before he'd had to touch her. And what had he done? Attacked her like a teen in heat. He grinned. She'd seemed to enjoy it. It had been almost painful to leave her with her lips swollen from his kisses and a flame of desire glowing in her eyes to return to the stage.

Now he was trying to focus on his music despite his attention continually returning to Michelle. Her eyes were always there to meet his. She had a slight smile on her face, which pleased him. Beautiful any time, Michelle was radiant when she smiled. Something she was doing more often now. She deserved to be happy.

The band finished their final number and said goodnight. Ty put up his guitar and shook hands with the other members. He searched the area where Michelle had been sitting and found her no longer there. After a moment of panic, he located her waiting near an empty booth across the room. With an excited skip to his heart he grinned and joined her.

"I saw this one open and thought I should get it before someone else did." She returned his smile.

"Great. You have a seat. I'll go to the bar and order those burgers. What would you like to drink?"

"A soda would be fine," she said as she slid into one of the bench seats.

Ty laid his guitar case on the other bench and made his way across the room. He hurriedly placed their order, worried that Michelle might change her mind and leave. Had he ever felt so insecure about a woman before?

Returning to the table, he said to Michelle, "Scoot over. Emily is taking up all the room on the other side."

She wrinkled up her forehead. "Emily?"

"Yeah. My guitar."

She moved further into the booth. "You named your guitar."

"Sure. Doesn't everybody?" He slipped in beside her, moving close enough that her thigh met his from hip to knee. If he could get away with it, he'd say forget the burgers and let's go home but was afraid he'd scare her off. He'd already come on too strong.

"I don't know. I don't play a guitar."

"Maybe I'll teach you someday." He picked up her hand and began caressing each finger. "With these long fingers I bet you could make lovely music."

She gently pulled her hand away. "Who knows? I might just take you up on that offer some time. Now, tell me what you were saying about a table here being named for my father."

"See that booth over there." He pointed across the room. "There's a little gold plaque on the table with your daddy's name on it."

"How do you know?"

"I was in here the other day and happened to sit at that booth. When I read the plaque I knew the Ross had to be yours." She looked as if she wanted to push him out of the way and go and have a look.

"I had no idea."

"I figured you didn't," he said.

"Why didn't you tell me sooner?"

"I don't know, maybe you pretty much told me that

you had used me and didn't plan to have any more to do with me."

She had the good grace to appear ashamed. "I'm sorry. I hadn't meant to imply that."

By the expression on her face, he believed she was. "I can't really blame you. I've never given you any indication that I wanted more."

Her eyes grew wide and she looked at him expectantly. "Do you?"

Ty tightened his lips and shook his head slightly. "No. I'll be leaving in three weeks. That's how it has to be."

She gave him a resigned look of understanding and looked away.

He needed to get them back on an even footing again, change the subject. "Hey, when that couple leaves we'll have a look."

One of the barmaids brought their meals and refilled their drinks before she turned to another table.

"I can't eat all this!" Michelle exclaimed. "This burger is bigger than I remember."

"I sure can. I'm starving," Ty said, picking up his burger from beside a pile of French fries.

Minutes later, with half his burger gone and Michelle well into hers, he said, "So tell me about your father."

He smiled as she wiped her mouth daintily. She was all lady, even in a bar and grill.

She finished a fry. "Well, he was an accountant with one of the banks here in town."

Ty looked at her. "That's what he did for a living. Tell me about him."

Her eyes held a solemn look. She blinked and leaned back into the corner of the booth. As if the words were water pouring out of a pitcher, she said, "His name was Alan William Ross. He played basketball in high school, he liked to fish, and loved to laugh. Fried chicken was his favorite Sunday meal. He wore suits when he went to work and refused to wear one on the weekend. He went with me to the mall one Saturday afternoon but he didn't come home with me."

"What happened?"

"He died of a heart attack at forty-two years old."

"I'm sorry."

"I am too." She looked around the room. "I miss him every day. He brought me here the Saturday he died."

"No wonder you haven't been back. It must have been tough to come tonight."

Michelle's look met his. "It was. In more ways than one."

"I'm glad you did."

"I am too."

Michelle straightened again, bringing her leg back into contact with his. Where it belonged. They ate in silence for a while. Ty enjoyed sharing a meal with someone, especially when it was Michelle. He was starting to discover that the loner life didn't have as much appeal has it once had.

"Now it's your turn," she said, eating her burger with more gusto than she had before. "You know about my family. How about yours?"

The last bite of his burger lodged in his throat. He forced it down. This wasn't where he'd been planning to go when he'd asked about Michelle's father. His parents, his past were things better left alone.

"I don't think you want to know about them." With a relief that knew no bounds, he watched as the couple that had been sitting in the booth they'd been waiting for left. "If you're done, we can go and look at that plaque now."

"Yes, I'd like that."

Ty watched as Michelle ran her index finger over the

gold-colored plaque on the worn wooden table. "Alan Ross sat here."

"Ty." She looked at him and said, "Thank you for this. I'll have to tell my mother." She slipped her hand into his.

He squeezed it. "How is she?"

"Doing better than she has in months. She's no worse for wear after her stay in the hospital. She's even starting to get out more. Maybe she has turned the corner."

"I sure hope so. Are you ready to go?"

"Yes."

"Do you mind giving me a ride home? My motorcycle is still in the shop."

"Oh, I can't believe I've forgotten to ask about your injuries. You don't seem to be favoring them anymore."

"They are all better. My palm is still tender but that's no big deal." He put his hand out to show her.

"When did you have the stitches taken out of your knee?"

"I took them out early last week."

"Figures," Michelle said with a curl of her lips.

"If you want to give them some TLC, be my guest."

"Do they need it?"

"No, but I do love getting attention from you. Especially if you're washing my hair," he said with a grin.

She lifted her shoulders and let them drop. "Maybe if you're on your best behavior…"

"How about that ride, then?"

Michelle smiled. "I believe I can give a stranded man a ride home."

The question was whether she would be willing to come in when they got to his place.

Michelle pulled the car into the parking space that Ty indicated. The apartment complex was as nondescript as any she'd ever seen.

Would Ty invite her in? Did she want him to? Would she go if he did? She'd been trying to answer those questions with every mile she'd driven.

"Thanks for the ride." Ty opened the door and maneuvered his large body out of the compact car. Going to the passenger door, he opened it, leaned in and retrieved his guitar.

Her stomach dropped. He wasn't going to ask her in. She watched as he started to walk away. Blinking, she put the car into reverse then pushed it back into park. Perhaps she should reach for what she wanted. She rolled her window down.

"Hey, you have any coffee?"

"Yeah. Want some?"

"Yes."

She joined him on the sidewalk and they strolled towards the building. They entered the open stairs area and climbed to the second floor. She followed Ty to the third door. He put his guitar down and slipped his hand into his pocket. "I was wondering how long it would take you to get up the nerve to ask if you could come in," Ty said with a grin before he pulled a ring of keys out of his pocket and placed one in the lock.

Had he been playing her? Was he so sure of her he knew she didn't want to go home? "What made you think that?"

"I don't know." He pushed the door open with his foot. "Maybe the way you looked at me while I was playing tonight."

"I didn't look at you in any way."

He chuckled while picking up his guitar and stepping inside. She followed him. He closed the door behind her. The only light was the one burning over the kitchen sink.

"Yeah, you did. Like you could eat me up."

"I did not."

"You did. Just like I'm going to do to you."

Michelle had no idea when or where he put down his guitar. All she knew was that Ty's arms held her tightly and his mouth had found hers. Her arms circled his neck. He eased the pressure and found a different angle so that his mouth more completely took hers. This time the passion between them soared. She shuddered against him. Her blood hummed with the heat that Ty generated deep in her. Tingling all over, her heart tap danced to the driving need he created. He pulled away. She groaned in complaint.

"I thought you wanted coffee," Ty said.

She cupped his cheek and brought his lips towards hers. "I don't even like coffee."

He looked at her with twinkling eyes. "Why Dr. Ross, if you're not interested in my coffee then what do you want?"

"You." Her lips found his.

Michelle woke to the smell of coffee and bright sun filling the window. She had slept well into the morning, a luxury she rarely allowed herself. Instantly she knew Ty wasn't near. The comfort and security she felt when he was around was missing.

She found his T-shirt on the floor, where she had dropped it after pulling it off him the night before. Slipping it over her head, she tugged it down. She inhaled deeply. His scent surrounded her. She had it bad for the man. Could Ty possibly feel the same way about her?

She padded barefoot out of the bedroom in search of him. As he'd taken her to his bed during the night, she'd not noticed much about his apartment. Out of the fog of desire she had only seen that it was furnished with the necessities only. There was nothing personal in it outside of Ty's clothes and guitar. Nothing permanent. Just like Ty.

For once she refused to dwell on the past or the future and live in the now.

She found Ty with his hip against the counter, drinking a cup of coffee. He wore nothing but his jeans. She'd never seen a sexier man on billboard or TV. When he saw her a smile slowly creased his face. The smile that was for her alone. Her stomach fluttered. Her ego was going to be a big as Ty's if he kept looking at her that way. She'd been wanton enough last night.

"Hey," she said softly, suddenly feeling shy.

"Hey, yourself, ma belle." He lifted his cup.

"Why do you call me ma belle?"

He chuckle softly. "Haven't you ever heard the old Beatles' song, *'Michelle'*? It reminds me of you. Pretty." His finger caressed her cheek. She leaned into his touch, liking the idea of belonging to him.

"Would you like a cup of coffee, ma belle?"

She shook her head.

"No, that's right, you don't drink coffee." He put the cup down and looked in the refrigerator. "Bottled water?"

She took the bottle. "Thanks. You travel pretty light."

"Yeah, not much room on a bike." He grinned.

"That's a fine-looking coffeemaker, though. Carry that on your bike?"

"Naw, but I request a good one to be supplied by the house service wherever I stay. Hey, how about we go to the beach for the day?"

She looked at him. "I can't do that."

"Why not?"

"That's hours away. I need to check on my patients. See about my mother."

"We can stop by the hospital on our way out of town and you can call and check on your mother. Come on, Michelle, for once in your life do something spontaneous."

A slow grin formed on her lips. "Okay." His look of surprise made her laugh.

"You'll go?" he asked, eyebrows raised.

"Yes. I'll go. Sounds like fun. How's that for spontaneous?"

"Perfect." He reached over and pulled her close for a kiss.

"Let me get a quick shower first. We'll need to stop by my place also," she said.

"I need a shower too. How about I join you? That way it'll take us less time."

She ruined the serious look she'd manufactured by breaking out in a smile. "I doubt that. I think you're hoping I'll wash your hair."

Ty gave her his best wolfish grin. "Among other things."

She gave him a look suggesting she would enjoy the "other things" as much as he would.

CHAPTER EIGHT

MICHELLE HAD TO admit that there was a feeling of freedom that came with saying yes to a spur-of-the-moment idea.

Her shower—okay their shower—had taken longer than she'd planned but it had been the nicest and most rewarding one she'd ever taken. She'd agreed to wash Ty's hair and in return he'd washed all of her. Afterwards they dressed and prepared to leave.

"I'm not riding two hours to the beach on your motorcycle," Michelle announced as she slipped on her shoes.

"My motorcycle isn't out of the shop yet. So you can cool your righteous indignation. I've arranged for a rental. I've gotten tired of bumming a ride. In fact, could you drop me off at the rental place? They've got my replacement in."

"Okay," Michelle said as Ty settled into the passenger side of her car after placing his guitar in the back. She liked that about him. Ty wasn't one of those men who thought he should always drive just because he was the male. He was comfortable with who he was.

"While I see about the car you'll have time to check in on your mom and call the hospital," Ty suggested.

He knew her so well. She needed to let her mother know she'd be out of town for the day.

Ty climbed out of the car with a wave of his hand and a "See you in a few" at the car rental place.

At home Michelle made her calls. She discovered that her mother had made arrangements to spend the afternoon having tea with a couple of friends at a local luxury hotel.

"You enjoy your day, honey," her mother said after Michelle had shared her plans.

Her mother had been acting more like her old self after her recent hospital stay. She'd even begun cooking again. A couple of nights during the last few weeks Michelle hadn't even stopped by to see her, at her mother's insistence. The awful thing about it was that it had been during the same weeks she hadn't seen Ty. The nights had been impossibly long.

She'd just finished talking to her mother when Ty knocked on the door and she let him in. He looked irresistible. She had to grin. He was hers for the time being.

"What?"

"Oh, nothing," she said, moving further back into her condo.

"How's your mother?"

"Amazingly well. She's going out to tea with some friends."

"I told you she'd be fine." His deep voice sounded like warm molasses.

"Yes, you did. It must be wonderful being a know-it-all." She turned and grinned at him.

He stepped closer giving her a gentle kiss on the lips. "You know, it's nice to see you smiling."

Michelle kissed him back. "You know, I'm really looking forward to spending the day with you. Hey, I need to get us some towels." In her room, she looked for her beach bag. It had been so long since she'd spent a day at the seashore she had to search for the bag. Locating it, she stuffed it with towels, sunscreen and a hat for herself before returning to the living room.

"I didn't know it took such a large bag for a bikini," Ty commented with a grin from where he lounged on the sofa.

"You're such a funny man, Dr. Smith."

"I don't find the thought of you in a bikini funny at all." His eyes took on a predatory look.

Warmth flowed through her. All it took from Ty was one special expression for desire to flame within her.

"Come on, we'd better go if we're going to get some beach time in. We'll take my car," Ty announced, reaching for the overstuffed bag she held.

"I was going to suggest we take my car."

He huffed. "It has all the trappings of the family van. If you're going to the beach you need to be in a beachy car. I have just the auto."

Ty had her curiosity aroused now. "What did you rent?"

"You'll see, but it's something that'll suit us both. Let's go. I need to grab my guitar out of your car."

Michelle preceded him out the door. They walked to the parking area, stopped at her car then Ty led her towards a black convertible sports car.

"You rented this! Why am I'm not surprised?" Michelle yelped.

"Yeah, I thought it might be the best of both worlds. Wind in the face for me and secure enough for the safety-conscious in you."

"You rented it with me in mind?"

"I did."

"But you weren't speaking to me."

"Yeah, but I was hoping you'd come round."

"Why did you think that might happen?"

Ty opened the trunk and placed the bag, guitar and his towel there. He turned to her. "Because I think we are good together. That you wouldn't want to waste what time we have together. I hoped you might come around."

So he hadn't been holding a grudge against her. Instead, he'd just waited for her to figure her feelings out.

"Come on." He shook the keys at her. "You want to drive?"

Michelle quirked her lips and took them from him. "You know, I believe I do."

She climbed in and secured her safety belt. With a chuckle he slid into the passenger side. She glared at him.

"What?" he finally asked with a raised brow.

"Buckle up."

With a playful look of disgust he jerked the belt across his waist and clicked it into place. "I'm ready when you are."

With a grin she cranked the car. Michelle maneuvered through the light weekend traffic and out onto the interstate. Applying gas, she appreciated the well-built fast car as they sped down the road.

"I had no idea you were such a speed lover," Ty said over the noise of the wind around them as they hit the open road.

She glanced over at him. "That's because you don't know as much about me as you think you do."

Ty reached over and placed a hand on her bare knee below her shorts. "I know most of the important stuff." He teased her skin with his thumb.

She pushed his hand away. "Don't distract the driver."

"Do I distract you?" he asked with a smirk.

"Too much," she responded without thinking. And he did.

It was nearing lunchtime when they arrived at the beach.

"Would you like to sit down somewhere to eat or would you rather grab a sandwich and eat on the beach?" Ty asked as they cruised along the shore road.

"A sandwich would be wonderful beside the water." Michelle stopped at a traffic light. While they waited she raised her face to the sky. "I'm so glad you talked me into this. Just having the sun on my face feels wonderful."

Ty took one of her hands and squeezed it. "You look magnificent." Ty reached over and kissed her.

The honking of the car behind them jerked them apart. They laughed and Michelle pulled away. A swirl of joy went through her. She'd just gotten caught necking at a red light. Had she ever done something so foolish? She smiled. This feeling was what it meant to be happy. Something that had been missing in her life for far too long.

"Pull in here." Ty indicated a deli that sat just off the road. She parked. Ty opened the door and said, "I'll run in and get everything we need. You just enjoy the sun. I'll be right back."

She watched as he walked away with his self-assured gait. He held the door for a woman and two children exiting the building. Ty smiled at them and said something that made them grin in return. Ty made people feel good. He made her feel special.

By the time Ty returned, she'd moved to the passenger seat.

"Hey, you're not going to drive any more?"

"I thought it was time for you to chauffeur me around for a while. I want to see the sights. I haven't been here since I was a girl. I can't see everything if I have to pay attention to my driving."

"Well, as long as I get a tip for my trouble."

"You have something in mind?" She gave him her best somber look.

"I do. But I don't think out in public is the right place."

She enjoyed sharing comments and secrets that were special just between the two of them. Ty was not only her lover but her friend.

"I know the perfect stretch of beach for us so you rubberneck to your heart's content."

"Have you been here often?" Michelle asked as she looked out at the ocean beside the road.

"Yes."

"Did you work in a hospital near here?"

"Not exactly," he said flatly.

Was he being evasive on purpose? "Is it some secret?"

"Michelle, just leave it alone."

She turned to look at him. His eyes remained on the road ahead. A muscle jumped in his jaw it was so tightly clenched. "Why did you bring me here if you don't like it?"

"I do like it. I just hate some of the memories."

Michelle understood that. She asked nothing further.

Minutes later, Ty pulled into a subdivision of six small beach cottages and then into the drive of one of them.

"What're you doing? You can't just park here," Michelle stated, looking at the storybook place in front of them.

"I'm not. I know the guy who owns this place."

Michelle studied the small but immaculate house. "Oh. Nice. Very nice."

"I thought you might like it."

"Come on, I'll show you around," Ty said pleasantly, as if his earlier mood had completely disappeared. They climbed the stairs to the white-painted rail porch. He placed a key in the lock of the bright blue door.

"You have your own key?"

"Yeah, I stay here sometimes between jobs."

"You don't own a place anywhere?"

"Nope. Never have."

Michelle was surprised. She couldn't imagine going through life being little more than a vagabond. They might be on the same page in bed but their book of life was entirely different.

Ty pushed the door open and let her enter ahead of him. The room they stepped into took her breath away. Windows covered the back of the house and beyond lay the white sandy beach and crystal blue ocean. The furnishings were done in nautical colors. It was a shiny and light room while at the same time a place of comfort. Michelle loved it immediately. "This is wonderful. It's just the kind of place I'd love to have for a hideout on days off."

Ty chuckled. "Come on, I'll show you the rest of the cottage. I think you'll like it too."

The house had three bedrooms. The two small bedrooms shared a bath. They were brightly decorated also. The master bedroom faced the ocean. There were ceiling-to-floor windows and glass doors that opened onto the deck that covered the length of the house along the back. It was as meticulously decorated as the rest of the place.

"It's perfect!" Michelle exclaimed. "You may have to force me to go home."

"You can stay as long as you like. Let's go to the beach. I'm ready for a swim. Why don't you change while I put our lunch in a cooler and get a couple of folding chairs?" Ty said, as he headed out the bedroom door.

Half an hour later Ty found them a spot in the sand. There were few people sharing the area with them as the beach was mostly used by the owners of the cottages. Occasionally people walked by along the ocean edge. Ty placed the two chairs side by side and put an umbrella up between them.

He had changed into swimming trunks that were navy blue with a yellow stripe running down each thigh and wore no shirt. He'd pulled on a baseball cap that controlled his hair but left his irresistible curls gathered along the back of his neck. Dark glasses covered his eyes. He could have been a lifeguard with all his tanned, honed muscles and good looks. She couldn't take her eyes off him.

He didn't even look in her direction when he said in a hoarse voice, "You know, if you don't stop looking at me like that I'm going to forget about spending time on the beach and take you back inside to the nearest bed."

Warmth that had nothing to do with the temperature filled her. "I wasn't looking at you."

He flipped up his glasses and gave her a direct look. "Yes, you were," he said with amusement in his voice.

"Are you calling me a liar?"

"If the shoe fits," he quipped as he adjusted his chair closer to hers and sat. "You can maybe make it up to me by going for a swim with me."

Michelle pulled the large T-shirt she was using for a beach covering off. She'd not worn a bikini, as Ty had requested, but she did feel like she looked good in the aqua one-piece. His low whistle didn't disappoint.

"I think you might look far sexier in that than in a two-piece. It makes me imagine all that beautiful creamy skin beneath." He threw his hat into the chair and grabbed her hand, pulling her towards the waves. "Let's go. I need to cool off."

They ran into the water hand in hand, laughing as it splashed against their chests. When a larger wave came toward them, Ty lifted her up to prevent her from being swamped. He let her slide down his wet slick body and stole a kiss.

Ty swam with strong, sure strokes through the surf, dove under and returned to where she trod water. He surfaced with a splash and shook his head, sending salt water into her face.

Michelle retaliated by shoving a handful of water in his direction.

"So you want to play that game," Ty said, his face a mask of mock evil, before he sent water her way. She shot some more back and war was on. Finally Ty plunged under the water, wrapped his arms around her waist and pulled her under. She came up sputtering and him laughing. Michelle turned her back to him as if she was mad.

Ty moved closer. "Hey, I didn't mean to make you—"

Michelle rounded on him and propelled two handfuls of water into his face.

"You sneak." He grabbed her around the waist again, pulled up and fell into the next wave.

This time when they came up, Ty didn't let go. Instead, his lips found hers. He requested entrance to her mouth and she gladly opened it. Her arms circled his neck and her legs looped his waist. He tasted of salt and life. When Ty broke the contact Michelle didn't immediately let go. His hands moved to cup her bottom under the water. She looked into his stunning eyes that so confidently returned her look and knew she was hopelessly in love. The pure, clear and forever kind of love.

Fear filled her. She let go of him and pushed away. "I'm worn out. I could use some sun time."

Ty didn't argue. He took her hand and helped her stand as the tide washed the sand beneath their feet away. Had she ever had more fun being with someone? But he wouldn't be there much longer. Her heart would break when he left. She slipped and his strong arms supported her, not unlike the way he had done over the last few weeks. He'd been there when she'd needed someone. It had become so easy to depend on him.

She plopped into her chair and he followed suit after picking up his hat. Ty shifted the umbrella so that most of their bodies were in the shade.

"We're both going to need some sunscreen," he said, pushing his wet hair back and pulling on his hat.

Michelle dug through her bag and came out with a bottle. She squirted a blob into Ty's outstretched hand. Planning to do the same in her own, it was forgotten when she got caught up in watching Ty apply the lotion across his chest.

"Hey, you'd better get that sunscreen on. With your fair skin you'll be red in no time."

Michelle refocused, burying a shard of hurt deep down, and started spreading the liquid over her skin. She glanced at Ty again, this time noticing how he pulled his hat low to shade his eyes. "I've been meaning to ask you where you get those ridiculous surgical caps you wear all the time. They're certainly not the usual ones offered in the supply magazines."

"You don't like them?"

"They suit you."

"That was a nice dodging of the question. They're made by the sister of a guy I worked with over in Virginia. His niece has cancer. A group makes and sells them as a way to raise awareness and make some money for his niece's treatments."

Michelle's mother was the one with cancer and Ty was doing more to speed the need for research than she was. "I see."

He reached over and squeezed her hand. "I didn't mean to make you feel bad."

"I'm fine," she murmured, and closed her eyes.

A few minutes later she turned her head and opened one

eye to find Ty with his eyes closed and breathing deeply. She shut hers and joined him in sleep with a soul-deep rightness that came with knowing he was near.

Ty woke to find Michelle still resting beside him. She looked peaceful, content for the first time since he'd met her. He'd not allowed her much sleep the night before. It had been so good to have her in his arms again.

She'd amazed him on the drive over with the aggressiveness and confidence she'd shown as she'd driven. He hadn't been sure she'd like the sports car, worried that she'd consider it frivolous and unsafe. Instead, she'd embraced it. He normally liked to do all the driving but he had to admit he found it nice to just sit back and enjoy the ride. Michelle took advantage of the limits of the car without overstepping the bounds of the law.

His stomach growled. It had been a long time since their rushed drive through breakfast.

"Is that you making all that noise over there?"

He rolled his head towards Michelle. Her eyes were still closed but there was a hint of a smile at the corners of her lips.

"As a matter of fact it is, smartypants."

She opened her eyes and grinned. "I'm hungry too."

"Then I'd say it's time for some food." He pulled the cooler toward him. Opening it, he removed a clear plastic-wrapped sandwich and handed it to her. "Ham and cheese on wheat or if you prefer it ham and provolone on a Kaiser."

"Ham and cheese on wheat sounds great."

He handed her the sandwich along with a small bag of chips and a can of drink. Then chose his own. They ate in silence for a few minutes.

"Ty?"

"Hmm?" he said around a bite of sandwich.

"Will you tell me why you got so upset earlier about me asking about you staying here?"

The food stuck in his throat. He had to force it down in a gulp. He should have known she'd ask. Michelle wasn't the type to pretend a problem didn't exist. "My family lived here during the summer sometimes." He heard her shift but he focused on the waves hitting the beach.

"So what was bad about that?"

"When I say lived here, I mean in a tent under a pier or in a vacant house.'

"Why? Did your father lose his job?"

Ty chuckled, the sound dry and bitter. "I've never known my father to have a job in the traditional sense of the word."

He'd told few people about his parents. In fact, he'd found it easier when he'd been in college and med school just to say they had died. But it felt good to be telling Michelle the truth. Saying it, having it out in the open was cleansing. Also he was sure the information wouldn't go beyond Michelle. Even if it did, did it matter any more?

"Something like that. My dad took seasonal jobs and occasionally my mother would also."

"So you've never live in a house of your own?"

"Not really. I stayed with my grandparents for a couple of years while I was finishing high school and after that there were dorms and a mattress on the floor, whatever I could find."

"I didn't know people still lived like that."

"You'd be surprised by the number of people that live their whole life as transients," Ty said as he watched a seagull work himself closer for some food.

"Do your parents still move from place to place?"

This was harder than he'd thought it would be. "I guess. I've not seen them in seven years. They showed up when my grandfather died. I don't know how anyone got in touch with them but there they were."

"You don't get along?" she asked in a low voice.

"It's not so much that we don't get along as it is that we don't share the same beliefs." Even though he answered Michelle's questions he still wasn't being as forthcoming as he could be, but he needed to say it and she needed to hear it.

"As in religion?"

"No, it's more that they don't believe in traditional medicine and I'm a doctor. They are not impressed."

"I'm sorry."

"Hey, it really doesn't matter."

"I think by your tone of voice that it does matter. It would matter to me. What my mother thinks is important to me." She said nothing for a few minutes. "So you decided at sixteen that you would become a doctor and went to live with your grandparents?"

"Something like that," he murmured.

"What're you not telling me?"

Michelle had gotten to know him so well, but he couldn't tell her about Joey. Couldn't admit that he'd let his brother die. "Nothing."

"Yes, there is. I can hear it in your voice."

His heart constricted and he let out a heavy breath. What would she think when he told her? How could she not think less of him? Be disappointed. "You won't let it go until you hear the whole sordid story, will you? If you must know, I had a younger brother. Joey had asthma. My parents thought it would get better with rubs and warm weather. After a while he got worse. My parents wouldn't take him to the doctor. Even though I thought they should I didn't say anything. Didn't make them take him. I was there when he drew his last wheezing breath. Now you know it all."

For a long time all he heard was the lap of the waves

against the sand and the scream of seagulls and relived the pain.

Michelle's hand came to rest on top of his, which lay on the chair arm. She stroked his fingers until he spread his so that hers weaved between his. For once in his life he felt as if someone understood his broken heart.

"I'm sorry. Truly sorry."

Ty turned his hand and took hers in his. "I am too."

They sat for a long time, neither of them saying a word. There was healing to just having Michelle's touch.

"You're getting burnt," Ty said. "Let's go in."

Michelle didn't feel like she was but she didn't question him. She put their leftover stuff from lunch into the cooler. Ty stood and helped her to her feet. She reached for the chair.

"Leave it. We'll get them later." He picked up the cooler and took her hand as they walked back to the house.

While passing through the kitchen, he placed the cooler on the island. He led Michelle into the master bathroom. She didn't ask any questions, seeming to understand that he didn't want to talk. He turned on the shower and guided Michelle under it. She didn't say anything as he stripped her suit off and then his own as they rinsed. Turning off the water, he snatched a towel from the rack and dried Michelle's hair then her body.

"There's a robe in that closet," he said, indicating a small door with his chin. He flipped the towel over his shoulder and pulled it across his back. Michelle put on a robe and handed him the other. He shrugged into his and followed her into the bedroom. She opened the door, letting in the breeze, and stood on the threshold. Pushing her damp hair away from her face, she looked out towards the ocean.

Ty came to stand behind her, wrapped his arms around her waist and pulled her back against him. There was something about holding Michelle that made the sadness of his childhood disappear. That made him think that, with her, happiness might be possible.

They watched as a spring storm darkened the sky and slowly rolled towards them. As the first drop of rain hit the deck, Ty stepped backwards, taking Michelle along with him. He kept moving until the bed hit him behind the knees. Letting go of her long enough to remove her robe and his, he pulled the covers back. Slowly they sank to the bed.

Hours later Michelle lay awake curled in Ty's arms, looking out at the ocean. His breath brushed her cheek each time he exhaled.

Their lovemaking had been extraordinary. The passion had been powerful, searing and exquisite. Ty had taken his time to bring her close to the pinnacle and had then held her there, only to let her slide down to send her upwards again. She had never felt more worshiped, cherished, as if he was making sure that she had no doubt who was loving her. Had he intended to brand her with his mark, ruining her for anyone else?

Still he whispered nothing about the future.

A few minutes later he woke up. She felt his lips on her shoulder and his length pressed against her bottom. "I have no strength where you are concerned," he uttered in a rough, sleep-laden voice.

She smiled. There was nothing like being wanted. It was a perfect moment and she sought to capture it and never let it go but she had her heart to consider. It would burst as sure as a glass shattering on the floor but she had to know. Had to prepare.

"Ty."

"Mmm."

"What're we doing?"

He kissed her earlobe. "You mean you don't know?" His fingers trailed along the curve of her hip.

She rolled over to face him. "I mean us. Where does this go?"

His eyes flickered with something she couldn't put a name to before he grinned.

"Ma belle, can't we just have some fun together while I'm here? Enjoy each other. See where that leads."

She already had an idea of where things would go. She'd be left behind to stitch up her gaping wounds while he rode off into the sunset on his motorcycle. But she couldn't resist him. She'd learned that life was too short not to grab happiness when she could. Right now she wanted to seize that with Ty. Live a little. No, live a lot. "I guess so."

He kissed her and made her forget about everything but the moment.

Some time later Ty said, "Why don't we stay here tonight? My case is the late one and yours is too. We could drive back early in the morning. We could eat fresh seafood and enjoy the sunset. What do you think?"

Why not? She'd decided to live some and today she was going to do that. "Sure. That sounds like fun. But we'll have to be on the road early."

"Sure thing." He had such a boyish grin on his face she was glad she'd agreed to stay. He gave her a kiss on the lips before he got out of bed. "I'll get what we need if you want to stay here and call your mother."

He knew her far too well. "That would be nice. I'd like to check in with her and the hospital."

CHAPTER NINE

TY LAY IN bed with Michelle curled against him. He lightly stroked her bare hip as she slept. The last few weeks had been wonderful. The best he could remember.

They had spent every minute together outside work. A number of times they had shared dinner with Michelle's mother at her house. The more often he sat in the cozy kitchen with the mother and daughter over a hot home-cooked meal the more those old feelings of the need to belong pulled at him.

Michelle had even joined him at Buster's when the band had played one weekend. There had been a number of curious eyes as they'd entered the bar but soon Michelle had joined the other staff members and blended in as if she had always been one of them. The two of them had even returned to the beach cottage for an entire weekend.

Michelle continued to give generously in her lovemaking and he'd rewarded her in return. The days had been nothing but pure bliss as far as he was concerned. Better than he deserved. But the nagging thought persisted that it couldn't last. He wasn't the guy to depend on, to trust when the going got tough. Michelle needed someone strong and sure who could be there for her no matter what came her way. She deserved that much.

"Hey, sleepyhead." He jiggled Michelle lightly.

"Hi, there," she muttered into his shoulder, which she was currently using as a pillow. He liked the fact she had to touch him when she slept. He found he liked a number of things about Michelle. If he had been a different man, he could be comfortable with her forever.

He'd sworn he wouldn't allow himself to develop those feelings. He couldn't let Michelle know how much he cared. It would only hurt her more when he left. Who was he trying to kid? It was going to be the hardest thing he'd ever done to leave her. But they both knew the deal. Michelle had made her choice. He'd been nothing but up front with her.

Once during the past weeks she'd asked, "Have you thought about maybe taking a permanent job somewhere?"

"Not really."

"What if one came open here? Would you consider staying?"

He'd kissed her and that had been the end of the conversation. She'd hinted a few additional times that she hoped he'd remain longer and he'd never made a comment one way or the other. He was dodging her questions, not wanting to take the joy out of their time together. Neither of them seemed to want to push a discussion about the future but it was racing towards them like a car at the Daytona 500 and it wouldn't be waved off.

"Ma belle, you know that Schwartz will be back in a week."

"I heard," she mumbled as she kissed the ridge of his jaw. Her hand crept lower on his middle. Her lips moved towards his mouth and that was the end of the conversation again. Maybe he'd resist longer next time.

Some time later they were sitting on the couch in Michelle's living room when she said, "I thought you were going to teach me how to play the guitar."

"Did I say that?" He hesitated.

She twisted toward him. "Yeah, you did. How about showing me now?"

On some level Ty wished he'd never mentioned it. The last time he'd agreed to teach anyone to play had been when Joey had asked. He'd just learned his first chord when he'd started getting so weak it had been difficult for him to practice. Still, Michelle gave Ty such an imploring look that he couldn't bring himself to turn her down.

"Get Emily and I'll show you a few chords," he said.

She uncrossed her legs. "I don't know how I feel about fetching another woman for you."

"Jealous, are you?" Ty quipped with a smile. After he'd chiseled through that thick cover of seriousness Michelle had built around herself, he'd found below a sense of humor waiting to see the light of day.

She gave him a smirk and headed out of the room.

With encouragement, Michelle had been willing to try something new more than once in the last few weeks. They'd gone indoor rock climbing. She'd agreed to go on a short afternoon ride with him on his motorcycle after it had been repaired. Now she was asking him to teach her how to play the guitar. It was as if she was trying to get caught up on all the things she'd missed out on since her father had died.

Michelle returned with his guitar. He stood and took the case from her.

"Have a seat." He laid the case on the low table in front of the couch and removed the instrument then came to sit beside her. Strumming the strings a couple of times and tuning it, he offered it to Michelle.

"Now, hold it this way." He placed the guitar across her thigh and showed her where to place her hand along the neck. He moved in close, their thighs touching, and put an arm around her until he could reach the strings. The other hand he placed over hers holding the neck. "Now, place your fingertips here and here, and hold the strings down. With your thumb…" he indicated the one over the base of the guitar "…strum."

Michelle did as he instructed then put her hand in the air and shook it. "That hurts."

Ty's heart constricted, forming a knot of pain in the middle of his chest. Those had been Joey's exact words and actions the first time he'd run his finger over the taut wires. It had been so long since Ty had let himself think about Joey, really remember the hurt and desperation and bone-deep guilt that had been part of his life for so long. Why was it now festering to the surface with such persistence?

"What're you thinking?" Michelle asked softly.

"Nothing," he murmured, making a slight shift away from her.

"I can tell by the look on your face that something is bothering you."

She always seemed to be able to do that. Every time he drifted into negative memories she was able to read his mood. No other woman had ever done that before. He'd never let anyone close enough that they could. Michelle had slipped past those barriers he'd carefully built and maintained like they never existed. He'd let her see things no one else had been privy to.

He looked at her. Michelle's eyes had a resolute but uncertain look, as if she feared what he might say. "I was starting to teach Joey to play when he died. He thought it hurt when he strummed too."

Michelle's eyes clouded over. "We don't have to do this."

"No, I want to. Joey would want me to show you how to play."

She gave him a reassuring smile. "Then I'll do my best."

Ty returned her smile. "Let's try it one more time."

The thoughts of teaching Joey had become a bitter-sweet memory. He had Michelle to thank for that.

The next afternoon the clerk called, "Dr. Ross," as Michelle went by the OR central desk. "Dr. Marshall left a message that he'd like to speak to you when you have a minute."

Michelle smiled and said, "Thanks for letting me know, Roger."

The man's eyes widened a second before he smiled. "You're welcome."

Roger had looked as if he was surprised that she knew his name. Had she really been so aloof? She'd noticed that after they had gone to Buster's that there had been more camaraderie in the OR among her team. They had been good together before but now they were seamless as they worked. She had to admit that it made for better patient care. Why hadn't she realized that sooner?

Michelle knocked on Dr. Marshall's door and heard him call, "Enter."

She'd not been in his office since she'd gone to complain about Ty the first day he'd been at the hospital. That seemed like a lifetime ago. Now she'd give anything for him to stay. She'd mentioned him leaving and he had too but they'd never really discussed it. Maybe if she ignored it, it wouldn't happen.

Ty cared about her. She felt it every time he looked at her, touched her or spoke to her. When they made love the feeling was more powerful than any other time. But did he care for her the way she did him? The one thing that she was sure of was that she loved him.

She stepped through the doorway into Marshall's office.

Dr. Marshall waved her closer. "I just wanted to run something by you before I make a decision."

Michelle sat in one of the two chairs in front of his desk. "What's going on?"

Dr. Marshall pulled off his silver rimmed glasses and rubbed his eyes. "Well, to start with, Schwartz isn't return- ing. He's decided to continue working with the foreign aid group. He's going to take the director's position. So I'm in the market for another anesthesiologist."

"Have you thought about asking Ty Smith?"

"He turned me down, even though he's great by all mea- sures."

Michelle sucked in a breath and held it. Feeling light- headed, she grasped the arm of the chair until the skin across her fingers turned white. She was bleeding emotion- ally. Her chest felt as if it was caving in on her.

Breathe. Breathe!

Heat swamped her and her lunch threatened to return. She squeezed her arms around her waist. Ty couldn't have made it clearer that he didn't love her. He'd been offered a way to stay with her and he'd refused it. And not even told her about it.

Pain so searing that it burned as hot as lava settled in her chest. She'd hurt when her father had died. She had been worried sick when her mother had been diagnosed with cancer but nothing compared to this torment.

Dr. Marshall continued, "I was wondering if you have any suggestions about who you might like to work with?"

"I'm sorry, I need to go."

"Michelle, are you feeling okay?" Dr. Marshall asked, his forehead wrinkling.

"I'm fine." She'd never been further from fine. "I'll think about it and get back to you."

Michelle didn't wait for additional questions. She bolted for the door before she broke out in sobs. Finding the near- est private restroom, she locked herself in and let the tears flow. A quarter of an hour later she stood before the mirror, looking at her puffy eyes.

What a fool she'd been. She'd let herself hope that perhaps she and Ty were building something permanent, special. It had all been one-sided. She'd been Ty's female distraction while he'd been in town.

That wasn't true. He'd been up front. He'd not once said that he was going to stay. It had all been her, wishing.

Well, it was all over now.

She stood straighter and pushed her hair into some kind of order. This too she would get through. She'd survived other devastating events in her life and she'd live through this one eventually. Ty not loving her wouldn't break her. It was time to call it quits between them and move on. She might as well start accepting it.

After dabbing a water-cooled paper towel around her eyes, she opened the door and headed towards her office. Thankfully her day was over. She picked up her purse and made her way out of the hospital.

Where was Michelle? Ty had looked in the OR, on the floor and had finally gone to her office. She was nowhere to be found. They didn't check in with each other but he didn't usually have this much trouble finding her. He finally punched in her number on his cellphone.

"Hey, where are you?" he asked when she answered.

"I'm at home," she said in a dead voice.

What was going on? Had she heard? "I thought we had plans to try out that diner over on 60th Street tonight?"

"I'm tired. You go on without me."

"Why don't I get us a to-go plate and bring it by?"

"No, thanks. Look, Ty, I just want to be alone tonight."

What wasn't she saying? Knowing how stubborn Michelle

could be, he wasn't going to get it out of her over the phone. "Okay. See ya."

Less than an hour later Ty stood in front of Michelle's door. He knocked and moments later Michelle opened it. She was dressed in one of his T-shirts, a worn pair of sweat pants and a bulky sweater. Nothing about her appeared like the well put-together professional she'd worked so hard to appear for so many years. Something was wrong, badly wrong.

"What're you doing here?" she snapped.

"Well, thanks for the warm welcome." He lifted the two white takeout boxes. "I brought you dinner."

"I told you that I didn't want any."

"And I thought you said that just so you didn't have to see me and I'd like to know why." He was making an effort to sound glib while inside he was tied in knots with worry that she knew the truth. He only had a little more time with Michelle and he wanted it to be happy. Her attitude implied that his wish might not be granted.

Michelle put her hands on her hips, her sweater falling open to hang loose. She wasn't wearing a bra and her nipples pushed against the thin fabric of the T-shirt. As he watched, they pebbled. In her mind she might be mad at him but her body was still responding. She must have noticed his gaze because she pulled the sweater tight around her and crossed her arms over her chest.

Ty followed Michelle's gaze as she glanced at the older couple walking in their direction on the sidewalk in front of her condo. Their faces showed interest in what was happening between him and Michelle.

She turned back to him and hissed, "Come in. I don't want to have this conversation in front of my neighbors."

Stepping back, she allowed him to enter, followed and then closed the door behind her. Ty continued on into the kitchen, setting the boxes down on the closest counter. He turned to find Michelle standing behind him in what could only be described as a warrior's stance.

"When were you going to tell me?" she demanded, her look boring into his.

"Tell you what?"

"That you were offered a job at the hospital," she all but shouted at him.

"I didn't think it mattered. You knew I planned to leave. I've tried a number of times to discuss it with you but you didn't want to talk about it."

She had the good grace to look away. "So when do you plan to call ahead for a coffee-maker, pack up your boxes and get on your bike?"

"Day after tomorrow."

She gasped, her face going pale. Her next words came out in a strangled voice. "That soon."

"Yeah." The word drifted off as if he hated to say it. His heart constricted in agony. He was hurting her. Just as he'd hoped he wouldn't do. He hadn't expected the depth of pain he'd feel knowing he had to leave her. That she wouldn't be a part of his life but he couldn't stay. That was for her sake. He was no good for anyone.

She stood back and studied him. "You are more like your parents than you think." There was a note of censure in her voice.

"I'm nothing like them," he said sharply.

"Think about it, Ty. You don't stay in one place. You're always running. You don't even really own anything."

"Don't you get it? If I stayed I'd end up failing you. I found that out a long time ago. I'd let you down. I did that once and I refuse to let it happen again."

"How do you know? You've never stayed in one place

long enough to see what you're capable of. You won't know until you try."

"I know," he said, with a surety as immovable as the Appalachian Mountains as he backed away from her.

She shook her head sadly. "You carry so much guilt over Joey. You were a kid. You couldn't have done more for him."

He made an aggressive step in Michelle's direction and bared his teeth as he spat the words. "I could have made my parents take him to a doctor. The hospital. I could have taken him myself. I could have asked someone for help." He bit the ugly words out. "You don't know anything about me. What makes you think I wouldn't let the same thing happen to you?" He pointed his finger at her. "I'm not good enough for you."

Michelle stood her ground proudly through his tirade. For that he had to admire her. A lesser person would have been frightened.

"I would never have taken you for a coward," she said with a tone of regret. As if she'd had a revelation, she continued in an even voice, "You're afraid to commit. You're making excuses not to. You're not afraid you'll not be here if I need you. You're afraid that you might get hurt if you are. You're running because you *do* care." She narrowed her eyes and gave him an earnest look. "Don't you ever get tired of running from the past?" She waved a hand around. "It'll never stop following you."

What did she want him to admit? That, yes, it followed him everywhere, never left him? He looked at her for a long moment. "You talk about me being a coward. Have you told your team how sick your mother has been? Have you confided to anyone outside of me in years? Hey, maybe that's the way you want it. You knew I'd be leaving so it would be easy to tell me. You wouldn't have to invest yourself in anyone. You are still mourning your father. Still trying to be the perfect little girl. Where has that got you? No friends, no life. No happiness."

She put her hands on her hips and glared at him. "You have some nerve…"

"Hey, you believe you have all the answers? I'm thinking that maybe you need to realize a few things also. Realize that you can't control everything. Your mother's cancer. Whether I leave or not. All you can control is you and your life. And you decided to close off people years ago."

Michelle's mouth drew into a thin line and her eyes widened as a stricken look covered her face. She blinked and cleared her throat before she said in a subdued voice, "That all may be true but that still doesn't change the fact that you are still trying to deal with not standing up to your parents. Not insisting they take Joey to a doctor. You went into medicine to help and that's all well and good.

"But you run around from one place to another like the masked hero doctor. Spreading your brand of medicine and happiness as a shield against dealing with your past. You didn't leave your parents' lifestyle behind, you just ran away from them. And the pain. No matter how great a doctor you have become, it can't bring Joey back. All you can do is live well and honor him. That much I have learned in the last few weeks."

Her words hurt. Cut to the quick. The strong, clear-minded and confident Michelle had returned with a vengeance and pinned him to the wall. "I care about you, Michelle, I do. That's why I have to go. I don't want to watch as disappointment fills your eyes."

"That's the biggest bunch of bull I've ever heard. You don't know what it's really like to care about someone. Not since you were sixteen have you stuck around long enough to find out. You're not fooling anyone but yourself. And

I'm not sure that you're doing a good job of that either. You don't care enough about me to stay and try to build a real relationship. You're taking the easy way out. Never getting emotionally involved."

He glared at her but she didn't slow down. "Maybe we're not that different after all. But I do know one thing, I want a man who will be beside me through thick and thin. You're right, you probably aren't that person."

A stabbing pain tore through Ty's gut with those words. Michelle had given up on him, had decided he wasn't worth the trouble.

"Well, I guess everything that needs to be said has been. Goodbye, Michelle." He headed for the front door, the take-out boxes forgotten, the food gone cold just like his heart.

CHAPTER TEN

TY PULLED THE motorcycle to a stop near the campsite. He'd been on the road for weeks and had covered five states in search of his parents. Traveling from one to another, he checked locations they'd frequented as a family years earlier. Each spot he visited held good and bad memories.

When he'd left Raleigh and Michelle, he gone to his next assignment, which lasted only two weeks, sure that he would move on as if nothing had happened. Michelle would forget him in time and he would remember her as a pleasant interlude during a work assignment. But that couldn't have been further from the truth. He missed Michelle with a pain so consuming that it was almost tangible. At work, he remembered the intensity of her eyes snapping at him over her mask. On his motorcycle it was her thighs pressed tightly to his as he turned a curve. The worst was when he played his guitar. She'd ruined the joy for him. Michelle was in his blood.

Trying to outdistance the growing grief that roiled in him, he'd not accepted the next anesthesiologist position offered. Instead, he'd decided to take some time off and travel. He'd ridden his bike far and fast, trying to clear his head and hopefully his heart of Michelle. That hadn't happened. If anything, he'd become more miserable. He was constantly fighting thoughts of what Michelle would think about the places he was seeing, wishing she was there to share them. The worst was that he worried she might move on and no longer give him any thought.

After another aimless day he had fallen into bed. Sleep had eluded him. In the early hours of the morning he'd given up and seen the situation for what it was. He was hopelessly in love. It was time to face the truth and do something about it. But he had to face the past before he could ask Michelle to share his future. If he was going to do that, he had to find his parents. The thought of doing so made his stomach contract but it still had to be done. Now he was parked at a camp in central Florida. He'd been told his parents were there.

Placing his helmet on the seat of his bike, Ty walked across a grassy area towards the mobile campers parked under the trees. As he approached, a man in ill-fitting clothes came out to meet him.

"Can I help you?" the man said in a gruff voice that held a note of suspicion.

It was part of the lifestyle to be distrustful of any outsiders. Ty found it ironic that for years he'd been an outsider. The one new to the hospital, the staff, the OR team. In those places more times than not he'd been welcomed.

"I'm looking for George and Miranda Lifeisgood. I was told they might be here." His parents had changed their last names long ago. They'd said they'd had left their old life behind and their last names as well. To his knowledge they had never legally married. Smith was his mother's parents' surname and Ty had taken it when he'd move in with them.

"Who's looking for them?" the man asked, glancing over his shoulder.

Had he been signaling to someone? "I'm their son."

"Son?" he asked, as if he didn't believe Ty. "Didn't know they had one."

"Are they here?" Ty asked with a note of frustration. The woman in the last camp he'd visited had been sure his parents were traveling with this group. Ty started to step around the man when another one came out from among the campers and headed in his direction.

There was something familiar about the man's walk. He wore clothes similar to those of the first man but this one had the bearing of a leader as he stalked across the ground. His curly dark hair was streaked with gray and hung freely around his shoulders. As he came closer Ty knew without a doubt that it was his father. He was an older version of what Ty saw when he looked in the mirror.

Ty's heart beat faster. All of a sudden he had the urge to turn and leave but he had to face his demons and that meant talking to his parents.

"George," Ty said. He had never been allowed to call his parents by anything other than their first names.

"Ty? Is that you?" his father asked, coming to a halt just out of touching distance.

Ty nodded. "Yes."

"What brought you here?"

So much for the warm family welcome. He hadn't expected more but it would have been nice. In reality he'd not treated them much better at his grandfather's funeral. "I wanted to see how you and Miranda are."

His father looked at him so long without saying anything that Ty feared he would reject him.

"Come, your mother will be glad to see you." His father turned and walked off, not waiting to see if Ty followed.

Ty stayed a few steps behind his father as they weaved in and out between campers that had seen better days. Children ran around barefoot and elderly women sat huddled together, speaking softly, as they passed. Where Ty had once been an insider he was now very much the outsider.

They finally reached a camper that was set a little off from the camp.

His father's deep voice called, "Miranda, come out here."

Ty's heart thumped harder against his ribs. He would've known his mother instantly. She had aged but done so gently. Her long wavy hair reached the middle of her back and was controlled by a red bandana. Dressed in a flowing multicolored shirt that reminded Ty of Michelle's bright home, shorts and wearing rope thongs on her feet, his mother looked like the quintessential beachcomber.

"What's going on?" she called, stepping out of the camper door and coming down the steps. She looked in his direction and said in a breathy voice of pleasure, "Ty."

"Hello, Miranda." Ty held his breath. Would she turn him away? His mother stared at him for a moment as if she couldn't believe that he was truly there. She wasn't the only one. Finally, she opened her arms and Ty walked into them.

"I didn't think I'd ever see you again," she whispered.

"I know."

She pushed him back to arm's length and studied him as if she were a fortune teller getting a reading. "You're well, I see, and here for answers."

Ty nodded. He and his mother had always been in tune with each other.

"Then come, sit and let us hear your problem."

His mother welcomed him as if nothing had happened. Was it that easy? Ty glanced at his father. He was moving folding chairs around so that they faced each other. His father hadn't been as friendly as his mother but he hadn't turned Ty away either. Obviously it had been he who had held the grudge, not his parents.

They all took seats.

"First tell us how you have been," his mother said.

Ty gave them the short version of his life but didn't mention Michelle. He felt that if he put his plans into words it might jinx them. They were too important to take that chance.

"How have you both been?" Ty looked from his mother to his father.

"We are well," George said.

His father had always been one for few words and apparently that hadn't changed.

His father's face turned serious. "So, Tyrone, tell us why you are here."

Ty didn't miss the implication that he wouldn't have come unless he wanted something. Did they really have no idea what burden he carried?

"I want to talk about Joey."

His mother flinched. His father reached over and took her hand.

Ty forged ahead. "I want to know why you wouldn't take him to a doctor."

"Because it is not our way," his father stated firmly.

So the answer hadn't changed.

"Joey could have lived if he'd only had medicine." Ty worked to keep his voice even.

"We had no money for doctors or medicine," his mother said in a wistful voice. Had she begged his father to help Joey?

"There are programs. We could have gotten him care. I should have gone for help."

His father let go of his mother's hand and sat straighter. He looked directly at Ty. "We did what we could for Joey. It was meant to be."

"Did you know that I feel responsible for Joey's death?"

"Why would you feel that way, Ty?" His mother sounded truly mystified.

"Because I should have made you do something to help him."

"We did all we could," his mother said.

Ty let out a sound of desperation. Nothing was different. Except that his parents had moved on. He was the one who was stuck in the past. "Would you have let me take him to the hospital?"

"No," both his parents said at the same time.

The mountain-sized guilt that he had been carrying around slipped slowly off him. They wouldn't have listened to him even if he'd insisted that Joey see a doctor. They were so set in their beliefs that they wouldn't have allowed him to take Joey.

"We take care of ourselves. We'll not let others tell us what we need to do," his father stated.

His father referred to the government. His parents didn't vote, didn't pay taxes so they didn't exist. They wanted to keep it that way. No matter the cost.

Ty stayed a while longer and they talked about the past. Before Ty left he had his parents agree to keep in touch. They would at least drop a postcard in the mail to let him know where they were from time to time. As they got older he could check on them, use his skills as a doctor to help them when they wouldn't seek it elsewhere.

No matter what Michelle thought, his life was very different from that of his parents. He shared some traits but in other ways he was thousands of miles away from them. Sadly, he and his parents would never be close but they were still his parents. He'd try to leave his guilt behind and build a future free of blame.

Michelle knocked on the door of her most recent patient's room. Mr. Jordon was a seventy-year-old man who would be in her OR for triple by-pass surgery first thing the next morning. She gently pushed the door open. Her patient lay propped up in his bed and appeared to be asleep. A white-headed woman about the same age as the man sat beside him, holding his hand.

Michelle rounded the bed to stand beside the woman. "I'm Dr. Ross."

"I'm Martha Jordon. Richard's wife."

"I won't wake Mr. Jordon. He needs to rest. I was just checking to see if he or you have any questions about the surgery."

"What're his chances?" Mrs. Jordon seemed to be forcing the question out.

"I won't lie. The surgery is an intensive one but we do them here all the time."

Mrs. Jordon glanced at her husband and when she looked back her eyes were glassy with moisture. "Richard is all I have." She sniffled. "We couldn't have children. So he's everything to me." A tear dropped to her milk-white cheek. "I had cancer three years ago and he nursed me through the horrible chemo. I can't lose him now."

Michelle's heart broke for the woman. She knew what it meant to be alone. That deep endless void that nothing or anyone else could fill except for the person missing. Glancing around, she found a spare chair and brought it alongside Mrs. Jordan's. Sinking down on it, Michelle took the older woman's hand and held it. For a long moment they sat, saying nothing. Human touch was enough.

Finally Michelle said, "Mr. Jordon is strong. He should be fine. You need to take care of yourself. He'll need you when he gets out of here."

Mrs. Jordon gave her a weak smile. "I'll be there for him."

Michelle gave the fragile hand in hers a gentle squeeze. "I know you will." She stood. "Now, I want you to go home soon and get some rest. The nurses will take excellent care of Mr. Jordon overnight and I'll be in to see you both in the morning."

"Thank you, Dr. Ross. You've been very sweet."

Sweet? Michelle couldn't remember anyone ever calling her sweet. Determined, a good surgeon, self-reliant, but sweet? She kind of liked having that adjective assigned to her. "Goodnight."

Mrs. Jordon gave her a small nod and turned her attention back to her husband.

Michelle left and went to the nurses' desk. "Who's Mr. Jordon's nurse tonight?"

The other nurses looked everywhere but at her before one said, "I am, ma'am."

Michelle smiled at the young nurse and watched as she noticeably relaxed. "I'd like you to call social work and see if they have a volunteer who could sit through surgery with Mrs. Jordon. She has no one else and she shouldn't be alone."

By the time Michelle finished making her request everyone at the desk was looking her direction.

"Yes, ma'am. I'll see to it. If there is no one, I'll come in. It's my day off. They're such a lovely old couple."

Michelle smiled and glanced back toward Mr. Jordon's room. "Yes, they are. Thank you…"

"Becky."

"Thank you, Becky."

Michelle walked down the hall to her next patient. She'd never done anything like holding a family member's hand before and had certainly never thought of who sat with them during surgery. It felt good to focus on helping someone else instead of her misery. Ty would have been surprised and pleased if he'd seen her. More than that, she was proud of herself. Ty may have left but he'd been a blessing in her life, encouraging her to break out of her shell and show that she cared. For that, she'd always be grateful to him.

She still needed to take one more step.

The next morning she entered the OR. Her team stood ready to go to work. They all looked at her expectantly. Instead of her usual "Are we ready to begin?" she said, "I'd like to tell all of you something."

Almost in unison their brows rose.

"I know I've been a bit rigid and at times difficult to work with." There was no argument. She really hadn't expected there to be one. "My mother has been fighting a difficult battle with cancer and I've been preoccupied with her care and prognosis. I've been deathly afraid that I might lose her."

Murmurs of concern greeted her that were so heart felt that Michelle regretted she'd kept her mother's illness a secret for so long.

"My mother had cancer a couple of years ago and is doing great now," said one person.

"My niece had it as a child. She had her first baby six weeks ago," commented one of the scrub nurses.

"My father has it now," said another.

"I'm sorry to hear that," Michelle offered.

"How's your mother doing?" the nurse at the end of the table asked.

"Very well. We're getting good reports but the fight isn't over."

Jane, who stood at her right elbow, said, "I'm here if you ever need to talk."

"Thanks, I may take you up on that some time." With a lightness in her heart she'd not felt in a long time, Michelle meant it.

"Now, we need to get Mr. Jordon patched up. He has a wife that's waiting for him to get better."

Everyone took their positions and waited for her to take the lead.

"Mark, why don't you put on some of the rock and roll you like playing before I get in here?" Michelle said in a teasing tone.

"Yes, ma'am."

When all looks settled on her, she raised her brows and said, "Are we ready to begin?"

Hours later, Michelle walked into the surgery waiting room. Mrs. Jordon looked haggard but glad to see her. She took a seat next to the older woman and took her hand. "Mr. Jordon came through the surgery well and he's doing fine. You can see him as soon as they get him settled in CICU. That will take a few minutes."

"Thank you, Dr. Ross."

Michelle let go of the older woman's hand and stood. Smiling down at Mrs. Jordon, she said, "You're welcome. He should be home and under your care in less than a week."

"That sounds wonderful." Mrs. Jordon looked over at the woman sitting two seats over and back to Michelle. "I understand you are the one to thank for Robin being here."

Robin must be the volunteer in the traditional hospital volunteer jacket.

"I just thought you might like a little company," Michelle said. "I'll see you tomorrow. Please get some rest. We all know what bad patients men can be," Michelle said, and smiled.

It felt good to know that she'd not only done her best for Mr. Jordon but for his wife as well. Ty had told her that if she'd just let others in that she'd no longer need him. He'd been wrong. She'd started letting people in but she still needed him just as much as she ever had. Would the ache ever ease?

The blazing hot days of summer were in full swing as Michelle pushed her way into the OR for the last time that afternoon. The last weeks had been difficult ones as she'd adjusted to Ty's absence. There had been no phone calls, emails or letters. Nothing. It hurt but he was a free spirit and she'd expected nothing less. But it would have been nice…

It hadn't been easy, still wasn't if she allowed herself too much time to think. She'd strived day by day to move on. She'd shared a shopping trip with a couple of the nurses who'd asked her about where to buy clothes. It had been enjoyable and they'd planned to do it again soon. She wouldn't exactly call her interaction with the nurses friendship but she was making a step in the right direction. It was a slow process, learning to open up, but she was making an effort.

Her mother was still seeing her doctors regularly and all the reports were good. Michelle continued to be pleased with her mother's efforts to recover. She went out more, spent time with her friends and otherwise required less of Michelle's time. The downside was that it gave Michelle even more time to wonder where Ty was and what he was doing, which left her gloomy. Thankfully her days were busy.

"Hey, everyone, are we ready to go? Whose turn is it to pick the music?" Michelle asked as she walked toward the surgery table.

Silence hung over the room for a second before Jane said, "I think it's yours."

"Then how about some of the classics?" Michelle took her place and looked toward the head of the table. "Are we rea—?"

Her heart stopped, jerked into motion again and kicked into warp speed.

The sparkling green eyes that held steady over the mask of the person in the anesthesiologist's chair she knew so well. They were the last thing she saw before she went to bed at night. They were the ones that burned warm and caring in her dreams. The ones she wouldn't mistake for anyone else's. The ones she had looked for every time she'd entered the OR but had never expected to see.

Ty.

His gaze held steady. Waiting. Questioning. Asking.

Her breath came in soft, short gasps.

Someone cleared their throat, making her remember to blink.

Ty's eyelids lowered too but when they came up again his eyes held that infamous twinkle. Her heart zipped faster. If she'd paid closer attention, she would have known sooner that it was Ty. He wore a hot pink scrub cap with gray elephants on it. Who else would wear a scrub cap like that? She knew all too well what his thick, wondrously curly hair felt like in her hands. The perfect touch of it running through her fingers.

Glancing at the others in the room, she could see that they were watching her closely for a reaction to Ty being there. This time it wasn't in uncertainty but in anticipation.

"I'm ready. By the way, I like your taste in music," Ty remarked with a hint of humor in his voice.

How like Ty to joke when her nerves were tied in a knot. What was he doing here? Why hadn't he told her he was coming?

"I've been led to believe that music soothes the savage beast," she said in a dry tone.

He chuckled behind his mask.

How could she be expected to do her job with him sharing the OR? How long would he stay this time?

Michelle took a deep breath and let it out slowly. She was a professional and she had a surgery to perform. Thankfully it wasn't a difficult one. Maybe this was the case she should let her resident take the lead on.

Ty glanced at Michelle more than once but she never returned his look. It was as if she was making a point not to acknowledge that he was there. Did that mean she wanted nothing to do with him? Or did it mean that she was so aware of him that she was afraid she might be distracted? He hoped with every fiber in his being that it was the latter.

Ty had questioned whether or not to agree to be in the OR without letting Michelle know first. He'd been assigned the case and there had been no time to speak to her. Michelle was a consummate professional and would always put her patients' care first. If he'd thought anything less he wouldn't have taken the case.

Thankfully the surgery wasn't a long one. As soon as the resident finished closing, Michelle was out the door.

Ty had to stay with the patient until he was settled in CICU. Then he'd go in search of Michelle. He would have to hunt for her. She'd been shocked to see him and she would have gone somewhere to regroup before she could face him. He hoped that when he found her she'd still want to have something to do with him.

After checking on the floor for her, he then went back to CICU. He was told that she'd come and gone. He called her but she didn't answer. Was she so mad at him that she would refuse to speak to him? A fist of worry squeezed his heart. Had he missed his chance?

Determined to make Michelle hear him out, he circled around by her office to see if she was there. If not, he'd go to her house and then her mother's if necessary. He tapped lightly on the partially open door to Michelle's office then pushed it wide.

She sat behind her desk, removing the wrapper from a chocolate cake roll. Her hand shook slightly as she worked. Maybe she wasn't completely unaffected by his return after all.

"Hiding from me?" he asked.

She pinned him with a narrow look. "No. And I didn't say come in."

"No, you didn't but I wasn't sure you'd invite me in if I'd asked."

"What're you doing here, Ty? I thought you were long gone."

"Disappointed to see me?" Michelle had slipped her armor on again. She was covering up her feelings and he wouldn't let her push him away but she'd make him work for it.

"I don't care one way or another," she said in a perfect tone of dismissal.

He stepped closer and studied the contents of the trash can. Looking at her, he grinned. "I think you might. What's that, your fifth cake?"

She threw the cake she held into the garbage. "How many cake rolls I eat is none of your business."

"I think the number might have something to do with me being back and that makes it my business. At least, I hope it does." He moved around the desk, propped his hip on the corner and looked at her.

She squirmed in her chair and didn't meet his gaze. "How long are you here for this time?"

He couldn't help but tease her. "You're not glad to see me?"

Lurching upwards, she stood and glared at him. "Oh, for heaven's sake. I've not heard a word from you in weeks.

Now you show up expecting me to greet you with open arms. What do you want?"

"You."

Michelle's heart thudded against her chest as her blood zoomed through her veins. Had she heard Ty right? "What do you mean?"

"Come on, Michelle, you're an intelligent woman. You know what I mean." He grinned. Reaching out, he placed his hands lightly on her hips and tugged her closer.

She resisted slightly but Ty increased the pressure until his arms encircled her waist. She laid her hands on his shoulders and arched back so that she could see his face. "You can't just waltz in here and act as if nothing has happened. What I want to know is how long you plan to stay. I can't deal with you always leaving."

He leaned forward, bringing his lips inches from hers. "Why not?"

"Because." It was killing her not to lean forward and meet his lips with hers.

His mouth continued to hover a hair's breadth from hers. "Maybe because you love me?"

"I don't love you."

"Well, that's too bad. Because I love you."

She floated on a cloud of pure bliss at the possibility of those words being true. Did she believe him? She so wanted to. Pulling her shoulders back so she could look into his eyes, she asked, "Really?"

Ty grinned. "Really." His expressive eyes reflected the truth of the statement. "Now, with that cleared up, I'm dying for a kiss. I've missed you, ma belle."

One of Ty's hands moved to cup the back of her neck. He brought his mouth to hers. She leaned into him and wrapped her arms around his neck, meeting Ty's kiss with one of her own. He nipped at her bottom lip and she opened for him. He wasted no time claiming her. His tongue dipped and parried, requesting her submission. Michelle willingly gave him everything. How she had longed for his touch. She moved closer, running her fingers through his hair, wanting all of him.

The sound of someone clearing their throat made them jerk apart. Ty made a rude remark under his breath and stood.

"Excuse me, Dr. Ross," the social worker said, looking embarrassed. "I did knock. More than once, and the door was open. I need your signature on this order before the patient can be discharged."

Heat warmed Michelle's face. She'd been caught passionately kissing a staff member and she didn't care. She straightened her bright blue sweater and reached out to take the paper the woman offered. Ty made a discreet move to stand behind her chair.

Michelle provided her signature with a flourish and gave the woman a wry smile. The social worker left quickly, without looking back. Michelle giggled.

Ty chuckled and came around the chair to stand beside her. "You got caught necking in the hospital."

"That news should be all over the building in less than five minutes."

"Do you care?" Ty asked with concern in his voice.

She smiled and stepped closer to him. "Not really."

Ty studied her. "You have changed."

"How's that?" she asked with a secret smile on her lips.

"There was a time when you wouldn't have wanted anyone to know your business. And look at the way you're dressed. By the way, that blue is very becoming on you."

She grinned at him. "Thank you, you silver-tongued devil. I have made some changes. Or at least I've been trying to. It's hard. I did tell my team about my mother. They deserved to know. I'm just sorry I didn't do it sooner. I had no idea so many of them have been affected by cancer. They have been very supportive."

"Is this the place where I'm not supposed to say I told you so?"

"It must be hard to be right all the time," she retorted.

"It is." Ty pulled her to him, taking her lips in a sizzling kiss. "That's not the only thing hard about me." His hand cupped her butt, bringing her against his length so that his manhood stood rigid between them.

"I think it's time we find some place private." He gave her a quick kiss.

"I'd like that."

"Get your purse," Ty growled.

She pulled it out of a drawer then he took her hand and led her out of the office.

"Where're we going?" Michelle asked in a breathless voice when they reached her car.

"Your place. I don't have one yet. I'll follow you."

Ty didn't wait for her answer before he stalked off in the direction of the motorcycle parking area. As she drove, Michelle glanced back at Ty, who followed her closely. Was he playing her again? It was one thing to want her, it was another to be around for the long haul. She'd made some changes in her life but the idea of having a special someone forever hadn't altered. Pulling into her spot in front of her condo, she saw Ty take the closest empty one to hers. She'd hardly stepped out of her car before he stood beside her.

He pulled her close, giving her a blistering kiss that was far too brief. "I've missed you. Got to have you."

She grinned. "I'm glad to see you too."

Ty took her hand and they walked to her door. As she unlocked it he said, "I plan to show you just how much."

Heat pooled low in her. She wanted him too.

They entered and Ty kicked the door closed with his heel. He gathered Michelle into his arms before she could put her purse down.

"I need you," he said in a raspy voice, "so much it hurts." His lips came down to claim hers in a soul-searching kiss. His hands roamed her body as if he was remembering every slope and turn. He pushed at her clothes, the tips of his fingers finding the sensitive skin beneath her camisole.

Michelle was on fire. All she wanted was to be bare beneath him. Their clothes littered the floor as they slowly walked toward, stumbled to and fell onto her bed.

"You deserve more than a fast tumble but I can't wait to have you," Ty said, his breath hot against her cheek. "I've already waited too long."

The low rumble of his desire-filled voice increased her need. Michelle opened her legs for him. His manhood came to rest strong and ready at her entrance.

Ty's gaze found and held hers. "I love you," he said as he pushed into her wet, waiting warmth.

"And I love you." She encircled his hips with her legs and welcomed him to where he belonged. Ecstasy enveloped her. She'd found her safe haven once more.

Ty reveled in the feel of Michelle's warm, luscious body nestled beside his. This moment, this woman were what had been missing from his life. He planned never to leave her.

"I think I'd like you to make love to me again really soon." She ran a hand over his chest, causing his skin to ripple in reaction.

He chuckled and caught her hand under one of his. "I think we need to talk first."

Michelle twisted so she could meet his look. "Since when are you the practical one?"

"Since it's time that I was."

She sat up, pulling the sheet with her, covering her breasts. Disappointment filled him. She had such lovely breasts. It was probably just as well. He needed to keep his wits about him. Pushing into a sitting position and reclining against a pillow, he faced her.

Her eyes turned thoughtful. "What changed your mind?"

"I found out real soon that life wasn't the same without you. I decided pretty quickly that I wanted you in it and if I wanted that I had to face my past, accept some things about it and myself." He paused and looked away for a second. "I went to see my parents."

Michelle leaned forward. "Oh, Ty, that must have been hard."

"It was, but it wasn't as difficult as I feared it might be. That's one of the reasons that it took me so long to get back here. I had to hunt for them. I rode from one end of the east coast to the other before I found someone who said they'd seen them recently." He crossed his arms over his chest. "My parents haven't changed. Aren't going to. They would've done the same for Joey today as they did back then. They wouldn't have let me take him to a doctor. I'm learning to accept that."

Michelle's hand cupped his cheek. "I know it won't bring Joey back but you make a difference in others' lives every time you step into the OR. You've made a difference in my life."

He kissed her palm. "Thank you for that."

She sat back and began playing with the hem of the sheet, no longer looking at him. "How long are you staying this time?" She glanced at him from under lowered eyelids, worry creasing her brow.

He ran a finger across her forehead, smoothing the furrows. "No time soon, ma belle. In fact, today was my first day as a full-time employee of Raleigh Medical."

Her eyes went wide. "Really?"

"Yes, really. I called Marshall when I decided you were right about me always running. I've decided I need to make a change in my life too. The job was still open and I accepted."

"Why didn't he say something to me?"

"I asked him not to."

She smiled. "So you'll be assigned to my OR regularly? If you are, you'd better show up on time."

"I think I've learned my lesson about that. But I'm not sure that I'll be assigned to your cases."

"Why not?"

He grinned at her perplexed look. "I don't know if Marshall will assign a husband to a wife's OR cases." He watched with joy and growing hope as uncertainty, amazement and then understanding moved across Michelle's face. "Will you marry me?"

She squealed and wrapped her arms around his neck. He kissed her with all the love he had in his heart.

Seconds later she pulled away. "Are you sure? You've moved around all your life. I don't want to be the reason you're unhappy."

"Ma belle, I've never been surer of anything. I've learned the hard way that you're what I want. I need to be where you are to be happy."

"You think you can live a conventional life?"

"I've already made a start. I bought the cottage from my friend. Well, he's more like my business associate. I'm a silent partner in Doctors to Go. Anyway, nothing screams stability like a mortgage."

Michelle observed him closely. "I'd say that's a start in the right direction. But I want you to be sure." She paused a moment. "Hey, why didn't you tell me you owned part of a business?"

He grinned. "Maybe I thought you might be a gold digger. Maybe I just didn't want to admit I was more of a conformist than I let on."

She leaned over and kissed him. "I don't think you'll ever be anything but unorthodox in a number of areas of your life, and I kind of like that about you."

"Really? I promise to conform enough to drive a minivan if you'll just have me and maybe a couple of my children."

"I'll have you any way I can get you. And I'd love to have your children."

"So," he raised a brow, "that's a yes?"

"Oh, that's a wonderfully perfect yes." Michelle sealed the promise with a kiss.

* * * * *

Mills & Boon® Hardback
January 2014

ROMANCE

MEDICAL

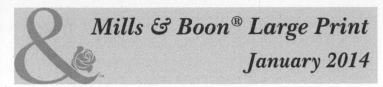

Mills & Boon® Large Print

January 2014

ROMANCE

HISTORICAL

MEDICAL

Mills & Boon® Hardback

February 2014

ROMANCE

A Bargain with the Enemy	Carole Mortimer
A Secret Until Now	Kim Lawrence
Shamed in the Sands	Sharon Kendrick
Seduction Never Lies	Sara Craven
When Falcone's World Stops Turning	Abby Green
Securing the Greek's Legacy	Julia James
An Exquisite Challenge	Jennifer Hayward
A Debt Paid in Passion	Dani Collins
The Last Guy She Should Call	Joss Wood
No Time Like Mardi Gras	Kimberly Lang
Daring to Trust the Boss	Susan Meier
Rescued by the Millionaire	Cara Colter
Heiress on the Run	Sophie Pembroke
The Summer They Never Forgot	Kandy Shepherd
Trouble On Her Doorstep	Nina Harrington
Romance For Cynics	Nicola Marsh
Melting the Ice Queen's Heart	Amy Ruttan
Resisting Her Ex's Touch	Amber McKenzie

MEDICAL

Tempted by Dr Morales	Carol Marinelli
The Accidental Romeo	Carol Marinelli
The Honourable Army Doc	Emily Forbes
A Doctor to Remember	Joanna Neil

Mills & Boon® Large Print
February 2014

ROMANCE

The Greek's Marriage Bargain — Sharon Kendrick
An Enticing Debt to Pay — Annie West
The Playboy of Puerto Banús — Carol Marinelli
Marriage Made of Secrets — Maya Blake
Never Underestimate a Caffarelli — Melanie Milburne
The Divorce Party — Jennifer Hayward
A Hint of Scandal — Tara Pammi
Single Dad's Christmas Miracle — Susan Meier
Snowbound with the Soldier — Jennifer Faye
The Redemption of Rico D'Angelo — Michelle Douglas
Blame It on the Champagne — Nina Harrington

HISTORICAL

A Date with Dishonour — Mary Brendan
The Master of Stonegrave Hall — Helen Dickson
Engagement of Convenience — Georgie Lee
Defiant in the Viking's Bed — Joanna Fulford
The Adventurer's Bride — June Francis

MEDICAL

Miracle on Kaimotu Island — Marion Lennox
Always the Hero — Alison Roberts
The Maverick Doctor and Miss Prim — Scarlet Wilson
About That Night... — Scarlet Wilson
Daring to Date Dr Celebrity — Emily Forbes
Resisting the New Doc In Town — Lucy Clark

 *Mills & Boon® Online*

Discover more romance at
www.millsandboon.co.uk

- **FREE** online reads
- **Books** up to one month before shops
- **Browse our books** before you buy

...and much more!

For exclusive competitions and instant updates:

 Like us on **facebook.com/millsandboon**

 Follow us on **twitter.com/millsandboon**

 Join us on **community.millsandboon.co.uk**

Visit us Online Sign up for our FREE eNewsletter at **www.millsandboon.co.uk**